The Grumpian Scythe

Buck Wilde

Published by Burn in Heck Press, 2019.

This is a work of fiction. Similarities to real people, places, or events are entirely coincidental.

THE GRUMPIAN SCYTHE

First edition. December 17, 2019.

ISBN: 978-1734270914

Written by Buck Wilde.

Acknowledgments

Edited by James Lee. Cover design by Damonza.

Satire Disclaimer

This fictional book is a political and social satire. It uses the names and likenesses of real people in mostly fictitious ways. Any resemblance to the truth is purely coincidental. The medical procedures described herein are not to be tried. They are entirely fictional and would not only fail to work but may result in serious bodily harm. The recipes included are fictional and should not be tried unless substitutes are made for bodily fluids, which should not be consumed by anyone.

Chapter 1 – "The Mad Emperor"

Having already announced the most important royals in attendance, Sean Spacer introduced the star of the show. "Lords and ladies," he began, "please rise for Emperor Donald J. Grump, First of His Name, the Chosen One, He Who Never Lies, Chief White Supremacist and Fornicator, and Master of his Domain. And Empress Telania, the Most Beautiful Woman in the World!"

A deafening roar surrounded me as His Majesty strode in with a broad grin, his combover no different than ten years earlier when he'd left the United State, but his jowls were looser, his paunch bigger, his hands smaller than I'd been led to believe, and his skin more orange than the last piece of citrus fruit I'd eaten. His extravagant robe had been embroidered with his name and title in fine silks and sparkling gemstones. His wife Telania heeled him, standing discreetly back in a gown that surpassed that of Princess Ivanaka, who looked on with thinly veiled jealousy. Everything about her attire and jewelry outshone her stepdaughter, whom she shot a look of superiority at and which Ivanaka pretended not to notice. Grump gestured for everyone to be quiet before he spoke.

"Lords and ladies, I am your emperor. I can have all of you killed in a moment's notice." Everyone laughed and I sensed this wasn't the first time he'd said this. He spent a few moments reminding people of those he'd executed recently, and while this continued, I gazed about the room.

Large pillars held up a vaulted roof that had been painted with the emperor's likeness as he reclined upon a cloud, one hand outstretched so that an adoring God could clasp it. Nude cherubs flew around him, beautiful women awaited his favor, and men knelt before him in submission. Similar scenes of subservience glowed in the stained-glass windows around the golden walls. Beneath these were multiple rows of throne-like chairs that paled in magnificence to that of the emperor himself. All were filled with lords and ladies of the realm, some of whom I recognized. Pucker Karlson. Shawn Handitty. Nick Nulvainy. Randy Pawl. Billy Barre. Lindsey Gramm. Devinn Noonez. The list could go on. Each wore a golden crown (smaller than His Majesty's), a massive diamond-studded ring on one hand, and brocaded robes. The men swigged foamy beer from rough-hewn metal goblets that, rather than accentuating their masculinity, augmented their femininity, in part due to the manicured hands and supple fingers that gingerly held them. They seemed unmindful of this as they snorted and sneered about them with such naturalness that I suspected none knew how disdainful they appeared.

The ladies were seated beside them but slightly farther back and lower, each draped in fine necklaces and elaborate dresses that raised their bosoms, their faces artfully covered in rouge, lipstick, mascara and the like. Most held crystal glasses filled with red or white wine, or champagne, behind which they tittered like schoolgirls. Zara Zanders. Kellianne Konway. Nic Hailey. Kierstyn Nealson. And more, plus the wives of the royal men.

All of them wore a vial of red liquid around their necks, or sometimes on a wrist, always on a gold chain. Curiosity had me dying to know what purpose they served.

"My lord," began Spacer, breaking my thoughts, "may I present to you Max Worth, Chief Reporter for Fox News, and Grump Loyalist from the Treasonous United Colonies."

"Hail Grump!" This unison, deafening roar came from every person in the room, save myself and the emperor, startling me with its vigor and volume.

Emperor Grump approached me and my handler, Svetlana, who stood beside me in the throne room. Before turning attention to me, he fondled her breasts, pulled her close, and thrust his tongue down her throat, right in front of Empress Telania, who frowned slightly. Svetlana squirmed but didn't otherwise resist, and when Grump had finished with her, he looked at me with smug satisfaction.

"It's good to be the emperor." He shook my hand, repeatedly yanking so furiously that he nearly tore my arm from its socket. "You can get away with anything."

"Of course, Your Majesty. It's uh, a great honor to meet you, sire," I stammered, trying to get my hand back. Grump wouldn't let go.

"You should try it. She won't resist you, will you dearie?"

Svetlana stopped fixing her mussed hair and blushed. "Of course not, sire."

"She's the best. The best. I only give you the best while you're here Max. You're a great man. Doing great work. I'm eager to hear all about what's happening back in that shithole country I used to run, from someone I trust. Are you loyal?"

I bowed. "Deeply, sire. I would do anything for you."

"You know I beat Crooked Hillary by ten points." This was his favorite nickname for the woman he'd defeated to become President.

"It was a great victory!"

As we stood there, a familiar figure in a black robe and cowl approached to stand next to Emperor Grump. Mitch McKonnell, the former United Colonies Senate Majority Leader, briefly conferred with His Majesty and then nodded at some instruction given to him.

"Have you met Mitch?" Grump asked me.

Confused, I stammered, "Um, no. I beg your pardon, sir, but I'd heard that you had died. I can see I was in error."

"Oh no," started Grump, grinning, "he's dead alright. He's now the Grim Reaper for real!"

As I looked on first in confusion and then amazement, the sallow skin of McKonnell's hideous face became something even more horrid, if that were possible. Skin melted away. Where once flesh had been, there now appeared only bone and two flickering pinpoints of orange flame for eyes, which gave off enough heat that I felt it bathe my face. A skeletal hand rose beside the cloak, and as if by magic or some unholy sorcery, a wicked-looking scythe appeared in his grip.

"Don't fear the reaper," came a hollow voice from inside Death's body. Then a burst of repugnant laughter chilled my bones.

Grump observed with a smile, "Now he kills people for me instead of just bills."

I smiled and couldn't help but ask, "Then why not send him after the U.C. President?"

"When the time is right."

I continued staring at the Grim Reaper. "How did this come to pass?"

Grump beamed. "I arranged it with an old golfing buddy." Muffled chuckles filled the room.

"Who?"

He cackled. "Satan!"

Indeed, Grump was more resourceful than I had heretofore imagined. Mitch faded from view in a puff of black smoke, on some unholy errand at our master's bidding.

Clapping me on the shoulder, Grump said, "Hang out for a few minutes. I have a few items to attend to." I nodded and he returned to the dais, seating himself on a golden throne studded with multi-colored gemstones. Svetlana guided me to a chair set aside for me and sat beside me as the crowd that had been behind us parted to let several individuals come forward. An armed guard led a haggard, unkempt woman before us, an equally filthy, female toddler in her arms. I wondered who the poor wretch was, but Spacey was soon to help us learn that very thing.

"You stand before His Majesty," he intoned, "Emperor Donald J Grump. What business do you have?"

The woman performed an awkward curtsy. "Sire, I am Olga Bella, a housewife."

"Well, you certainly didn't come from my GOP Rooms," Grump interrupted, causing laughter from the attendees. I didn't understand what he meant.

Olga bowed her head. "Yes, Your Majesty. I am not worthy. My daughter is very ill and may not survive without additional assistance. I have come to seek your help."

He arched an eyebrow and looked down his nose at her with cold disdain. "Are you saying that I don't provide adequate medical care for my people?"

"No, Your Majesty, that is not what I meant at all."

"That sounds like what you said. Isn't that right?" He glanced at the crowd, who murmured agreement.

"I beg your pardon, sire. That was not my intent."

He waved her off. "Well, what is wrong with her?"

"She has cystic fibrosis, Your Majesty."

"Cystic what? Sounds disgusting. Is your daughter attractive?"

"I, uh, I..."

"I, I, I," Grump mocked, rolling his eyes as most of those present laughed. "Bring her up here."

A guard yanked the girl out of the mother's arms and unceremoniously stood her up before Grump, who looked her over like a piece of meat as the guard pulled her hair back and turned her head from side to side.

"Hard to tell under all that grime. Ugh, she smells, too. Yeah, I don't think this is worth much."

Spacey spoke up. "The intervention is expensive, Your Majesty, and would require repeated visits at our premium hospital, reserved for us, the Inner Party. Life expectancy isn't very long. This isn't exactly going to pay for itself and they have no money."

The woman spoke up. "We gave our life savings to you when we arrived on our Golden Cruise, Your Highness."

Grump considered as if she hadn't spoken. "I don't see how they can pay for that and it hardly seems worth the trouble. I assume caring for the child places a burden on the household. One that I can ease. I've made my decision."

Olga bowed in gratitude. "Thank you, Your Majesty."

"Mitch!" he called.

A cloud of black smoke roiled the air beside the girl and the figure of Death stepped from within it. The little girl looked up uncomprehending but fearful as the scythe hurtled toward her neck and her mother screamed in realization. With the sound of metal slicing bone, the girl's head flipped into the air before landing with a splat and rolling away. As the body fell, Death's skeletal hand snaked forth to ensnare a white, glowing soul that briefly dangled from one finger before he rolled it into a ball, tossed it in the air, and swallowed it whole on the way down. After a moment, he let out a satisfied belch, which caused room-wide laughter that drowned out the pitiful wailing of the girl's mother, who guards led away.

Without preamble, another guard led a skinny, disheveled, unwashed man before the emperor as those assembled made no secret of their disgust. He stopped with tearful eyes on the little girl's body, the head just feet from him and looking toward him with wide eyes and mouth agape in a permanent expression of horror.

Grinning, Spacey asked, "Who are you and for what reason do you stink up this great hall?"

The man hesitated amidst the laughter before speaking in a timid voice. "I beg your pardon, Your Majesty. I am Donald Farmer."

Grump interrupted. "Were you named after me? You seem too old."

He bowed. "I changed my name in reverence, Your Majesty."

"Well, I'd be flattered if you weren't so disgusting. As it is, I think I'm offended." More laughter followed this but quickly faded as onlookers saw the muted disdain on the emperor's face. He was serious.

"Yes, Your Highness. We have few facilities to improve ourselves."

"So, you're saying this is my fault? I'm thinking to call in Mitch."

Visibly trembling, the man hung his head. "No, my emperor. It is the fault of the Treasonous United Colonies for stealing our wealth, as you have often told us."

"Hail Grump!" The shout echoed around the room.

"What do you want?" Grump barked.

"I come for your glory, Highness."

"Good start. Keep going."

"The workers want to work harder for you, sire, and if we had more food, we could enrich our empire faster."

"Our empire? Don't you mean, *my* empire?"

"Of course, Your Majesty. I only meant that we take pride in raising you higher."

"So, I am not high enough for you, is that it? I think I've heard about enough. What village are you from?"

"Grump Estates East, sire."

"Spacey, cut their rations in half. Mitch! Cut *him* in half."

Death once again appeared. As the man lost his bowel control, Mitch sliced him from crotch to the top of his head. The two halves fell to either side, a pile of organs and entrails steaming in the middle.

An exasperated but amused Grump remarked to the Grim Reaper, "I meant side-to-side, not down the middle."

Mitch bowed. "Begging your pardon, sire. You had not specified."

Grump waved him off. "Don't go anywhere. We have one more."

The last victim was dragged against his will before the emperor, who saw this resistance and didn't even bother learning his name or what he wanted. He just frowned and nodded at Mitch, who cut the man side-to-side.

Suddenly we heard a commotion from the entrance as someone tried to enter, excitedly saying there was very important news the emperor should hear immediately. People were pushed aside as the messenger made his way forward, out of breath, and eyes wide with excitement. His demeanor convinced any naysayers to be silent and let him speak.

"Your Majesty," he began, still gasping, "I have the most incredible news!"

"It had better be to interrupt us. I'm in a killing mood." Laughter filled the room.

"Yes, sire. We've shot down a fighter plane."

A murmur spread through the crowd. Grump asked, "A fighter plane? From what country? Better not be Russia or North Korea!"

"No, sire. It's from the Treasonous United Colonies!"

"Hail Grump!"

The messenger continued. "And we captured not one, but two pilots!"

Grump rose. "Two? That's wonderful news. Just wonderful."

"There's more, sire. One of them is black."

Grump frowned. "Well, we can always use more slaves." Chuckles went around the room. "Maybe we'll think of something special for this one. He's alive?"

The mention of slaves surprised me. I hadn't known they existed here. I tried to keep the concern from my face, wanting to learn more.

"Yes, sire. Both are alive. The other is a blonde woman, and you'll never guess her first name."

Always devoid of imagination, Grump just looked at him blankly, not even trying to guess. "I like blondes," he noted.

"Her name is Hillary Delosi! She's related to Nasty Nancy Delosi!"

A moment of surprised disbelief crossed Grump's face before he began to smile, then finally laugh as the crowd joined him doing so. A chant of "lock her up" began as Grump stood beaming, basking in the adulation. This went on for a long time before he finally gestured for everyone to quiet down.

"Where are the prisoners now?"

"They're being prepared for you to meet them, Your Majesty. They suffered minor injuries from parachuting to the ground. I was told it might be an hour and someone will come at once to let you know."

Grump considered and seemed pleased. "I have others matters to attend to in the meantime." He looked at me. "Come Max, fill me in on what's happening back in the Treasonous United Colonies."

"Hail Grump!" Again, the shout startled me as I rose to join him, Svetlana by my side. As we walked out together, he looked back over one shoulder and made one final remark to the crowd.

"You know I beat Hillary by thirty points."

"It was a great victory!" they shouted, clapping or raising their drinks in celebration. Then we exited the throne room.

Earlier that morning, I had arrived in Grumpland by plane, a guest of His Royal Highness for the coming fortnight. My TV show back in the U.C. had become a favorite of Grump and his only source of information from outside the island. He trusted no one more highly than myself, for he'd taken all of the opinion show hosts at Fox at the time with him so that my meteoric rise to the top echelons had come easily. And from that lofty perch I had extolled the virtues of His Majesty with such fervor, dedication, and relentlessness, that every month, thousands of loyalists would gather up all their wealth and board a Golden Cruise for these hallowed shores.

And yet I had never seen this place. So, at long last, I had been invited to be the first foreigner to visit and then report back to the world the gloriousness that is Grumpland. He'd promised to show me all the great secrets that no one outside this place knew. With me reporting on these other delights, surely even more Republicans like me would flock here each month to fill Grumpland with the citizens needed to take over the world. My role filled me with such excitement that it nearly overcame me at times. Grump's vision for a better world for me and my kind would soon reign unchallenged, unfettered by law, convention, or stupidity. Here there would be nothing but unending glory and riches for us.

It had been nearly ten years since His Majesty had left to build his empire in the Atlantic, where another great civilization, that of Atlantis, had once similarly left all others behind...before the sea swallowed it, jealous as it no doubt was as to the wonders therein. I felt certain the same fate would not befall Grump's promised land. Surely God would not devour *two* civilizations that could rival heaven? Atlantis must have allowed some evil to exist on its shores, but Grump? How could someone so holy commit evil?

Upon my arrival by plane, clouds and fog obscured the earth below me so that I saw little but the airport as I landed. Since I flew aboard Grump One, the plane arrived on his premium airstrip, reserved for His Majesty and his most preferred guests. I stepped from the cabin into the cool air, which was warmer than expected, though I'd read that in summer, temperatures can reach fifty degrees. Only now did I see that the runway had been painted to resemble a red carpet, but as I descended the stairs to the tarmac, a real one had been rolled out for me. Awaiting me at the bottom was my handler.

A blonde, blue-eyed femme fatale named Svetlana gazed up at me between long lashes. Her full breasts strained at a tight, white top, unbuttoned to show a generous amount of cleavage, nipples clearly visible beneath its thin silk. Grump had outlawed bras; they interfered with ogling. So, too, with panties, which interfered with his preferred way to grab a woman. She wore a black miniskirt and matching high heels. A pearl necklace graced her lithe neck, while diamonds dangled from each earlobe. As I came within reach, she took my hand in hers and pressed against me, a sexual invitation highly suggested by her demeanor.

"You are Max Worth?" she purred, leading me toward the nearest entrance.

I smirked. "So, they tell me."

"Come." She smiled, perfect white teeth gleaming. "Emperor Grump is eager to meet you. We have a full and exciting day planned. You will begin by meeting members of the aristocracy and then have a private audience with His Majesty."

"I'm honored and flattered."

"We're also expecting a Golden Cruise to arrive this afternoon. It's one reason for the timing of your visit. It's a great celebration, with the emperor as MC! What could be better? The ceremony takes place in front of the palace in Grump Square, so you'll see the preparations when we arrive."

"I've seen Golden Cruises depart but never had the privilege of seeing their arrival."

"I'm sure you will love it. They sell all of their possessions before they come, even the clothes they aren't wearing, for they know His Majesty will provide for and take care of them. He is their shepherd. They bring their entire life savings with them to store in Grump Bank, where they know it'll be safe, and where Emperor Grump will turn it into gold in time, making them far richer than ever before. He's great at the art of the deal. No one is better. No one."

I nodded, my eyes wandering to the golden trappings all around us now as we stood inside an immaculate airport lounge. Polished marble reflected the gold-tinted windows, mirrors, and metal surfaces. Luxurious fabrics covered plush divans that sprawled beneath crystal chandeliers. Richly stained woods adorned the walls, broken only by the occasional pictures of His Majesty, resplendent in robes and crown.

"There's more than just citizens on the ship," she continued, our footsteps echoing as we walked by waiters with champagne and little treats for me to savor. "We have slaves, too. We capture them from all over but especially shit hole counties. And Amnesia. That's mostly for revenge. They don't make the best slaves. Too lazy and they cry a lot when whipped. But the Africans and Mexicans, they're real workhorses. Much stronger. They're used to suffering. They're savages."

I sipped my drink, eager to hear more. "So, they're all minorities, then? No whites, I assume."

"Well, almost. We take white Democrats from Amnesia for sport, mostly. But most of the slaves are one of four groups: blacks, gays, Latinos, and Muslims. The gays are mostly white but they're still subhuman."

"No Kurds?"

"No. He got them all killed, remember?"

"Ah, yes, I had forgotten."

"They should've supported the U.C. in World War II."

I nodded, aware that the Kurds had done exactly that, a fact that had only gotten in Grump's way until he ignored it, as any clever man should.

"Later this week will be Hillary Fest," said Svetlana, breaking my thoughts.

"Hillary Fest? I'm surprised I haven't heard of this before."

"We like to keep things secret here, until now. It's an annual celebration of the emperor's victory over Crooked Hillary in the 2016 election. This is not to say that he waits until then to celebrate, but this is the official party where the population is allowed to join with him in victory. We construct a large wicker representation of her and, at the festival's finale, burn it."

"That sounds great. I can't wait to see this. Tell me, do I detect a Russian accent?"

"You do. I'm a gift from Mr. Poohtin to our dear comrade."

"Is it true what they say? That the Russians and North Koreans purchased Greenland, now Grumpland, while his lordship was still President of the United Colonies?"

"Indeed. They acquired it for him, sensing the need. With his majesty's failure to alter the U.C. Constitution to allow for more terms as president, it became apparent that he'd need a new home to carry out his mission."

I remembered recent history well. With Denmark owning Greenland and unwilling to sell it to the United Colonies, Russian and North Korea, two stalwart allies of His Majesty, had first blockaded and then bombed the ever-living shit out of Greenland. Denmark had always been full of pussies and were unable to mount a defense. Indeed, they'd only held a press conference and begged the pathetic United Nations to intervene. The UN didn't and Greenland was no more. And when Grump was out of office, and an evil Democratic, new President vowing not to pardon his supposed crimes, he and his devoted followers had journeyed to Greenland.

Not everyone, of course. The island was too small for all of his adoring throngs. Only the wealthiest donors had been allowed to enter the new Holy Land, Grumpland. The Land of Plenty. The Land of Enduring Freedom. The Land Without Fake News. The Land of Eternal Whiteness. I could go on and on and on. It was a Blessed Place, one foreordained by God, where religion infused every part of public life. No more separation of Church and State. No, they were one and the same! We'd find no Muslims here, and certainly no Jews! Only white, heterosexual, wealthy Christians!

After the War That Grump Won, he'd built his empire. With allies providing military might, Grump built naval, air force, space force and army bases, capturing former U.C.-held Thune base and converting it for his own use. His Majesty built the capitol New Grump City, Grumpolopolis, Port Grump, and a host of other towns along the major coastal locations. A huge wall – a thousand meters tall! – was being built to surround every inch of the land, so that no immigrants (or undead) could possibly enter without valid paperwork. Grump is both Master of the Wall and King in the North!

The other delights of his empire I would see firsthand, but as I walked beside Svetlana, I felt the need to freshen up. She led me to a bathroom, and I closed the door behind me before admiring the huge room. Everything was gold and diamond-studded. TVs hung on every wall so that no matter which way one faced, it could be watched, and after another step into the room, the motion detectors turned each of them on, providing my first glimpse of Grump TV. This was just one part of his own Grump Media conglomerate. Not seeing the remote, I wondered how to change the channel and finally took a chance.

"Change channel," I said aloud. Grumpland was rumored to be full of cutting-edge technology that far surpassed the United Colonies.

"Comrade," replied a female voice from all around me, "as you are a visitor, this first transgression will be forgiven, but you should know that there are no other channels available on Grump TV. A recording of your voice request has been sent to the Grump Ministry of Truth for storage."

I blanched, hoping I had not already ruined the esteem in which I was held. I lifted the toilet seat and saw the visage of Hillary Minton painted inside the bowl, smiling mouth agape as if to eagerly accept an offering. She'd been Grump's opponent in the 2016 Presidential election in the United Colonies, and Grump loathed her still. As I pulled out my member, the vantage point made it appear as though I were putting it inside her mouth. My copious pee stream hit the target perfectly after a moment of calibrating my aim. The toilet self-flushed and I turned to the sink, which turned on automatically. When I placed a hand under the soap-dispenser, which was shaped like a nude cherub with Grump's face, a diamond-shaped dollop fell from its butt onto my hand. A quick dry of my hands and I then noticed a warm towelette that I briefly placed on my face.

When I put it back, my watch struck the golden wall and left a white streak through it. I rubbed my finger on it, hoping to remove it, but I felt a groove in the wall where the damage remained. On closer inspection, I saw the reason. The wall was gold plated, not made of solid gold, of course, and I had scratched right through this. No amount of buffing by me would repair it. Hopefully no one would realize I was the culprit. There was nothing I could do about it, so I left.

I soon found myself sitting beside Svetlana, her hand on my inner thigh and creeping upward with each caress, as we lounged inside a golden limousine that comfortably cruised toward the palace. My eyes picked out the street signs as they went by: Grump Boulevard, Grump Scenic Byway, Grump Highway, Grump Avenue, Grump Circle, and so on. In the distance, as the fog began to clear, I saw the makings of a great pyramid that seemed to easily rival those of ancient Egypt. Nearer was a tall mountain with several heads carved into its lofty heights, but I couldn't make them out. To one side of the port, a golden statue hundreds of feet tall stood with one leg to either side of the lagoon's entrance, a sword in one hand and four decapitated heads dangling by their hair in the other. Seeing my curious look, Svetlana informed me they were representations of blacks, gays, Muslims, and Latinos, and that the

Grump Colossus was one of Grumpland's Eight Wonders. At this point, she seemed no longer content to let me stare out the golden window in silence.

"When was the last time you made love?" Svetlana asked, resting a cheek on my shoulder.

I tore my eyes from her boobs. "I'm beginning to feel like I never have."

She giggled. "You're very sweet."

"Not quite like yourself."

"His Majesty has decreed that you are to be treated like royalty while here. That means you needn't go without love-making."

I smiled. "What if you're not my type?"

She playfully rolled her eyes. "But I am. It doesn't matter. Every female on the island is yours for the taking."

My eyebrows shot up. "Really?"

"Yes. Just like the other royals."

"Even royal women are available to me?"

"Should you like."

"All of them?"

"Yes. From Queen Telania on down."

It couldn't be true. Could it? Well, it *was* Grumpland.

"We recognize that men are superior to women here," she continued. "We serve at our master's pleasure and are happy to know nothing and be provided for by our strong, virulent men. Our job is to give our master everything he needs to be even stronger, whatever form that support takes, whether cleaning the home, cooking for him, sexually satisfying his needs and desires, and even letting him take out his aggression on us, as it pleases him."

Startled, as this defied everything I knew of Grumpland, I wasn't sure how to respond to this and was saved from needing to as we turned onto Grump Way, where two golden gates swung open to admit the vehicle. We passed down the right side of a gilded avenue, where fountains shot water into the air, timed to Wagner's "Ride of the Valkyries." Manicured bushes and flower gardens lined the avenue. Elegant men and women strolled along in tuxedos and fine dresses, servants lingering nearby and carrying refreshments in case anything at all was needed.

Then the car entered Grump Square, the closest most people came to the palace. The square was a wide plaza lined with a low marble wall, atop which stood statues of the aristocracy, none more imposing or as tall as the one of His Majesty with a crown atop his head and his emperor's robe pulled about him. The statue's expression bore a look of naked disdain for those who would look up at it. One corner of this square had a permanent stage built into it, from where His Majesty conducted the welcome ceremony we'd see later that day. Otherwise, he typically made announcements from the lofty position of the palace balcony.

The car headed that way now, passing through more gilded gates and another manicured lawn before turning to stop at the covered entrance. A brass fanfare rang out into the cool air as we stepped from the limousine. Before us stood a palace so golden that even the windows had been tinted with gold. It gleamed in the sun as rays broke through the fog, sparkling like a jewel in the rugged landscape that surrounded it. Like something out of a fairytale, fanciful spires and minarets soared into the sky, decorative crenellations adorned the walls, and streamers and pennants fluttered in the cool air. I only realized I was staring when a grinning Svetlana pulled me forward, remarking that this was to be my home during my stay, in majestic guest quarters that were close to the royal suites. Before we entered, I glanced behind and saw the town below, where residents were able to see their emperor's lavish home looming above them.

Once inside, we passed lords and ladies on our way to an audience with His Majesty. It had been brought to my attention that this gathering was especially for myself, but only so I could report on the splendors of Grumpland back to the rest of the world. It wasn't personal. I enjoyed it, nevertheless, feeling myself grow confident and commanding, such that I soon led Svetlana instead of the other way around, wearing her upon my arm like a conquering hero. Down gilded halls and through sumptuous sitting rooms we strolled, a small crowd of well-wishers accumulating behind us until we entered a truly enormous throne room.

A murmur swept through them as Svetlana and I sauntered toward a raised dais where several empty thrones awaited. Not until we stopped, the crowd behind us ten steps back, did everyone get quiet and turn respectfully as if expecting something. From behind the thrones, a familiar figure danced into view, a ruffled, pink shirt open to his navel as he performed for those assembled, finally stopping before us. I recognized Sean Spacer from his days speaking for President Grump.

Spacey grinned at all of us. "Good morning, lords and ladies of the realm. I am your humble servant, here to announce the royal family and important nobles." He turned expectantly to one side, from where the first of those to arrive would enter the dais. After each person stepped on the stage, he spoke their names and titles while the crowd applauded until the individual sat on their throne. Only the royals would adorn the stage. The others would take seats closest to them.

"Duke Rash Limbaw of Gapingmaw, Minister of Outrage and Lord of Grump Radio." The Duke wallowed in slowly, whether this was to prolong the applause for himself or just due to his massive girth and wobbling legs. He was sweating profusely by the time his bulk plopped onto his throne with a groan that I couldn't tell the source of, himself or the chair.

"Duke Ted Spoogent, Master Entertainer, Fornicator-in-Residence, and Head of the National Gun Association." Unlike everyone else, Ted stepped onstage disheveled, robe open at the front to reveal that he was naked except for a soiled loincloth. He snickered with every step, ogling any woman who caught his eye.

"Duke Steve Bannun of Whitesonley, Minister of Cultural Solidarity and Honorary Ambassador to Scandinavia." Still looking like he'd had one too many shots, Bannun hardly acknowledged the crowd as he took his seat.

"Why honorary?" I whispered to Svetlana.

She answered, "Denmark claims we stole Greenland from them and neither they, Sweden, Finland, or Norway will let our ambassador on their shores."

Neither will the rest of the world, the bastards, I thought to myself.

"Duke Roody Jeweliani of Sesspule, Minister of Shadows and Multispeak." Roody sauntered in waving with first one hand and then the other, grinning broadly. He appeared to be talking to himself, but then I realized that after every sentence, he'd turn his head slightly as if addressing an invisible figure on first one shoulder, then the other.

"Duke Mike Pince of Succop, Royal Fluffer." This resulted in a snicker throughout the crowd and Spoogent adjusting his crotch. Pince, ever willing to please, walked on stage making sucking sounds, to the delight of the crowd.

Svetlana whispered in my ear, "He's privately called Duke Suckoff. He's known for devotion to His Majesty. Others used to compete with him but finally relented, recognizing Pince's superhuman traits in this regard. No one does it better than him. No one. Even those from the GOP Rooms have tried to learn his secrets to no avail."

I didn't have a chance to ask what she meant about GOP Rooms, as it was time for Spacey to introduce the royal family. He began rattling off the names of minor Grump family members like Prince Barron, now a grown man. I had noticed that the importance of the introduced individuals had been steadily rising, and so it came as no surprise when the next son was announced.

"His Royal Highness, Prince Eric, Minister of True News." A blond man strode in, not bothering to conceal a sneer of disdain and resentment. He stopped before his throne, looked me up and down, snorted in derision, and then sat, assuming a look of regal aloofness. I wondered if I had somehow offended him.

"Her Royal Highness, Princess Ivanaka and Prince Jaryd. Mistress of Fashion and Minister of Finance." Her face a tightly controlled mask of feigned serenity, the princess moved smoothly on glass, high-heeled pumps that peeked out from her elegant dress. A tasteful collection of jewels adorned her earlobes, neck, wrists, and fingers. She took a moment to stride back and forth before everyone like a runway model at a fashion show before finally extolling everyone to purchase similar items from her latest fashion collection. Then she joined her husband, who had been playing pocket pool and didn't seem inclined to stop, even when she held out one hand for him to take and arched an eyebrow that he hadn't yet done so. What most struck me was that Ivanaka appeared to have not aged a day since I'd last seen a report of her a decade earlier.

"His Royal Highness, Crown Prince Donald J. Grump, Junior, Hand of the Emperor, and Heir to the Throne!" The emperor's firstborn son walked in slowly, a rich, fur-lined robe spread as he opened his arms expansively, as if to suggest he owned everyone present. A not-so-secret smile of superiority graced his pursed lips and his chest puffed out importantly. He seemed to bask in the applause, coming to stand before everyone for a full five minutes while they praised him. You'd think he'd done something more noteworthy than being pushed out of his mother's vagina before his siblings. Finally, he turned and sat on his throne, on the right side of his father, either not knowing or not caring that his smile was really a sneer of contempt.

It was at this point that the emperor was introduced, greeted me, and then killed three citizens who'd come to seek his favor. But now he and I, Svetlana trailing behind us, walked away from here to do our interview.

As we went, Grump talked excitedly about the captured pilots, saying it was news he wanted to share with everyone immediately, so we made a pitstop on the way to our interview. It was time for an announcement, which he normally did on TV for big events, but he didn't want to take the time to get set up for that, so we were headed to the radio room. The facility looked like a typical radio broadcast room, though this one had a picture of both Grump and Rush Limbaugh on the wall. A smart technician had already anticipated the emperor's desire to do this and had turned on the needed equipment.

I didn't listen as Grump made his announcement, which wasn't long, because Svetlana pulled me aside to tell me a few things. Chief among them was that Grump was sometimes unavailable to make an announcement and others would do it for him. The catch was a device that made someone sound like Grump's voice. She pointed out which dial it was, saying that Grump sometimes used it himself when he had a cold so as not to project weakness. When I asked if the room was guarded to prevent misuse, she rolled her eyes, pointing out that only the Inner Party had access to the palace, aside from the slaves here, and no one would dare make an unapproved announcement. I suspected she was right, given the sudden executions I'd already witnessed. Grump ruled by fear, just like he always had.

With Grump's announcement complete, we moved a few doors down to a private sunroom with lush divans and wall-to-ceiling windows on all sides, providing a gorgeous view of a manicured garden and nearby mountains and valleys. Like everywhere, polished marble adorned the floors and it looked like no living person had ever set foot here, for it was utterly immaculate. As Svetlana waited outside, waiters discreetly stood in attendance, trays of snacks and drinks at the ready. One opened what looked like a Diet Coke soda can, but instead of "Coke" written across its side, it read "Grump" despite otherwise having the same logo.

We spent a few minutes talking about how much he loved my show before he gave me multiple chances to praise his invitation, the plane, the airport, his palace, and his handling of the audiences he'd granted earlier. I worried about saying the wrong thing, lest my biggest concern become which direction Mitch split me in half. I'd always been a keen observer and chose my words carefully. I hoped to raise the esteem in which I was held, not lower it. Before long, he got to the point – learning just how far the United Colonies had fallen since he'd left. I'd provided a steady diet of tidbits from my show, always dropping hints about worse to reveal, and he'd invited me here partly to learn it all.

He leaned forward. "So, tell me, comrade. They tore down the wall, didn't they?"

Chapter 2 – "The Interview"

"Yes, Your Majesty," I replied. "They tore down not just the parts of the wall that you built, but all of it. Even the section around Colorado."

Grump looked incredulous. "The southern border is completely open?"

I opened my mouth to deny it but sensed that telling him things he didn't want to hear wasn't a good idea. "Yes. Immigrants just pour over it."

"It's probably so bad that Texas is part of Mexico now. Terrible. Just terrible. The U.C. is a shit hole now. All those rapist Mexicans. Drugs. Rape. Incest. More guns and they wouldn't have lost Texas."

"Guns solve everything."

"They really do, comrade. They really do. I've always loved guns. Everyone should have one. What's going on with the NRA back in the U.C.? I heard it was gone."

Again, that wasn't true, but I didn't admit it. "Yes, effectively, the laws are more restrictive so that the National Rifle Association might as well be gone."

"Is it true that all guns have been confiscated from even law-abiding citizens? That's just what the awful Dems wanted! How are people supposed to defend themselves?"

Trying to lighten the mood, I replied, "With political correctness, sire?"

Grump blinked in surprise but didn't get the joke. "What? What does that even mean? If a criminal is trying to rob you or kill you, you're supposed to show them compassion? Say nice things to them? Forgive them. Turn the other cheek. What a crock of shit! For Christ's sake, whoever thought of such a thing? Do they think that bullshit works?" He seemed oblivious to having invoked the name of the very man who'd invented the idea.

"Apparently."

"Violent crime is at an all-time high, from what I heard. The Dems. It's all their fault. Everything's their fault. They were very weak on crime. Everyone should be well-armed to protect themselves. Or people can just take advantage of them."

"Absolutely agree, Your Majesty."

"You should see the guns we have here. It's real space-age stuff."

"I would love to see them."

"You're gonna love. Love it."

"And all of your people have guns?" I was hoping to stop talking about Amnesia to minimize the number of lies I had to let him believe.

"Oh no, we can't have that. They surrender their guns when boarding the Golden Cruise to get here. We keep my proles safe and under control. They don't need their own guns. I keep them safer. No one can keep them safer. No one. They trust me. All they have to do is tell us what they need, and we give it to them." The comment startled me because he'd just kill two people who'd told him what they needed. "Only the Inner and Outer Parties have guns, and lots of them. We hunt on the Safari all the time. It's great."

"Those in the proletariat don't hunt then?" I knew before arriving that the wealthy one percent was the Inner Party, while the Outer Party lived in more modest means but still had a good quality of life. By contrast, the proletariat, or proles, were the poorest and the ones whose living conditions I was more curious to see. Then there were the slaves, of course, but I hadn't known about them until this morning.

Grump shook his head. "No. Can't have the proles hunting. The penalty for proles having a weapon is death. It's over quick. On their knees and pop. To the back of the head. I'm good to my people. I only torture the ones who commit crimes, but no one ever does that. We don't even have laws."

"You don't use Mitch for this?"

"Nah. I was just showing off earlier. Besides, he gets everyone in the end anyway."

"If people don't have laws, how do you control them?"

"Fear."

"Do they know what they should be afraid of?"

"Yeah, me. Do a good job and everything will work out fine. Make me richer and I'll protect you. Screw up and you're done for. I have spies everywhere, even living among the slaves, so people never know who to trust. They know the spies are everywhere. It keeps them on edge. It's good for them. And me."

"Very clever." I wondered how much stress they were under, always being watched that way, never knowing who might turn them in for something, anything. Did they know what happened to those who came to the palace asking for something and never returned? I wondered how I could find out what they were told.

Grump nodded. "So, what about California? Still part of it? That's a shame. There's a state you could've gotten rid of. Let the rapists have their fun with those liberal Hollywood types.

They'd deserve it. They'd totally deserve it. Should've voted for me. You know I had the biggest crowds at my rallies there. Bigger than Crooked Hillary."

"Of course, sire."

"You'll see one of my rallies later. The crowds are just bigly."

"That's great."

"Drugs are just pouring into the U.C. now, aren't they? The Dems wanted open borders, terrorism, high crimes, and rape every day. Every day. Gotta love the Dems."

"They're terrible people, Your Majesty."

"They're enemies of the United Colonies. And me. They got what they wanted. They cry out to me to help now, but no way, comrade. No way. Gonna nuke them when we're ready."

I wasn't certain he had nukes, but some reports had suggested it. As I lived there, the idea of being obliterated by a nuclear bomb naturally concerned me. "How soon, sire?"

"Hard to tell. We got plans. We got plans. We got a wall all around the island. It's very, very... it's 5,000 pounds of concrete. Very hard. You know it's very... it's got steel, too."

"Steel is good." I sensed the opportunity to get an answer about the nukes had passed.

"It totally is! I love steel. We got alligators in front of it. Snakes, too. Giant water cobras. The most poisonous snake in the world. Grows to twenty feet or more."

I was pretty sure snakes wouldn't survive the cold climate but knew better than to correct him. Alligators were likely a problem, too. "Impressive! How tall is the wall itself?"

"Over a thousand meters! It's the tallest wall in the world. It's number one."

"Very impressive."

"Number one! It's got these anti-climb thingies. Even professional climbers can't get over them."

"That's great. Who is it designed to keep out, specifically?"

"Everyone. We're very strict. We have a travel ban on almost everyone. No immigration. Especially Vikings. Denmark wants its land back. We took it fair and square. Everyone says so. Everyone. They can't walk to our country. We have lots of water in between our country and them."

I couldn't argue with that. "Pardon me, sire. I thought you like Nordic types?"

"Well yeah. Blond and blue-eyed is the best. It's just the best. But we can't have Viking raids. They're rapists, you know?"

"Rape is bad."

"It totally is. It totally is. I mean, unless I'm doing it. Then it's good. It's good to be the emperor."

"I can't imagine."

"I'll show you later. You'll see."

"Um. Okay."

"Comrade, women love it. They really do. They're not good for much else. You're gonna love our national anthem when you hear it. It's just the best. Everyone says so. Ted Spoogent does an amazing job. Just amazing. He's a great supporter. It's almost a religious experience."

"I can't wait to hear it. Since you mentioned religion, what's that like here?"

"We're all Christians. Every last one of us. It's the state religion. We won't allow anything else, especially Muslims. Well, we've got them for slaves. That's all they're good for. Did the Dems really ban all religions after I left? They lie so much. Can never tell what to believe. Fake news everywhere! I bet Islam has taken over the country. There are mosques on every corner. Statues of Ali everywhere."

I wasn't sure if he'd mispronounced Allah or if he actually thought Mohammad Ali was their prophet. Not sure what I say, I kept it simple. "Yes, sire."

"I guess women have to wear those awful headdresses? That's terrible. Well, not for the ugly ones. I mean, who wants to see that? I bet you have terrorists running around all the time."

"It's a travesty."

"Let me guess, there's a mass shooting every day. And no one can stop them because only criminals have guns. I bet a thousand die in each one. The illegals are bringing guns across the border. Stupid Dems! They wrecked the country. Knew that would happen when I left. Everyone said so."

"You were right, Your Majesty. You were right."

"What happened to all of the churches? Someone told me they've been turned into brothels. That's not so bad, actually. I mean, I *like* brothels."

Again, I couldn't believe what I was hearing. I thought I was his only source of information. Well, then again, *accurate* information. He was getting lies from *somewhere*.

He asked, "Others have been turned into gay bars? Ugh! That's terrible! Terrible. The gays are just sick, sick people. We're working on a cure. Karson says he'll have it any day. You know, windmills kill lots of birds."

I blinked at the subject change but tried to seem unfazed. "Of course, sire."

"What's the rumor I heard about abortion clinics in churches? What's that about? Abortion is now required? I heard all women must have one by the time they're eighteen. What if they're not pregnant? Someone told me a local black stud gets to rape them until they're pregnant. Just sick. It's disgusting. They're animals. Just animals. But then the Dems are just as bad. Serves them right. What happens to the baby? You can't have these disgusting half-breeds."

"Uh, I'm not sure, sire." Honestly, all of this was stunning misinformation. I wondered if people were just making stuff up and the rumors were spreading, being repeated so often that they believed them? I didn't know what to say and opted for mostly going silent and avoiding outright lies where I could.

He said, "I think I know. I think I know. It's never born. And the fetus is aborted and then harvested."

"Harvested? For what?"

"Well, I heard that some are sacrificed to Satan, but I don't believe that one."

That was a relief. Part of me was surprised there was something he wouldn't believe. "Why don't you believe it?"

He leaned forward. "I think he would've told me."

Not hiding my confusion, I asked, "Who?"

"Satan. We're golfing buddies. I think he would've told me, but maybe not. He is the Father of Lies. I got a great golf course, just great, down in hell. In fact, it's called Hell-a-Lago after my old Florida estate. The final holes are right by the Lake of Fire. You'll never guess how many holes it has!"

Questions and disbelief swirled in my head (Satan was real? They were friends? There was a golf course in hell, which was real?), but since he'd asked a direct question, a response was at least easy this time. "Nineteen, sire?"

He chuckled. "Six hundred and sixty-six!"

"That's impressive." I wanted to laugh now, thinking he was joking with me, but he'd never shown a sense of humor in his life and nothing about his demeanor suggested he was kidding – unless he had the ultimate poker face.

"You bet. We should play a round before you go."

Smiling a bit, I asked, "Ah, don't I have to be, um, dead, sire?"

Grump shook his head. "Just damned."

"I see." The thought occurred that this might've explained how he was getting there, but I still respected him (this was waning) and frowned at my wayward thought. "Well, Your Majesty, I'd be honored to join you." And likely terrified if it was real.

"I heard that another use for the murdered babies is research. The Dems do all sorts of hideous experiments."

"I should look into it and report on it, on my show."

"You totally should, comrade. That would go over bigly. Democrats are always wanting to look younger. Raw stem cells are rubbed onto people's faces. It's literally aborted fetus cream."

"That sounds... gross."

Grump shook his head. "I have no words. No words. But there's something even worse."

"How can something be worse?"

"You need to look into this one bigly. I heard they're also turned into dietary supplements called Fetufu."

"What?"

"Gummies. The Dems, they take these gummies twice a day. They're made from aborted fetuses, which are turned into a kind of tofu. That's where the name comes from. They come in different flavors. Forbidden Apple Cinnamon, Passion Pomegranate, Bloody Mary. Most are shaped in a fetal position."

I stared at him. Where in the world was he getting this stuff? I mean I hated the Democrats, too, but this was monstrous. Did he and his people really believe this stuff was going on back in the United Colonies?

"From your reaction," he began, "I guess you haven't heard of this? That's too bad. I was hoping you might have some. I'd love to try one of these gummies. You know, just to see."

"Um, of course, sire."

Before he could say anything more, Kellianne Konway stepped into the room without knocking and promptly knelt on a divan, her skirt hitched up. Then she got on all fours and looked seductively at the emperor, her shirt unbuttoned enough to reveal sagging, shriveled breasts that she gently shook side to side. I couldn't help looking, sort of like when you pass a bad car accident on the highway and know you just need to stay in your lane and drive on.

"Your Majesty," she began, batting her eyes, "the prisoners are ready to be interrogated."

Showing no reaction, Grump stood up. I did as well. He put a hand on my shoulder. "Max, I need to go see these prisoners myself, but I have something I want to show you personally before I have Svetlana give you a tour of the palace."

"I'd be honored."

"Follow me."

Leaving a pouting Kellianne behind, he led me into the hall, Svetlana falling in behind us, as we continued through more gilded halls of gold, diamonds, and luxurious tapestries, furniture, and rugs on immaculate, designer stone floors. My eyes bulged at the beauty and a beaming Grump smirked in approval. After several twists and turns, we approached an open doorway with diaphanous silk stripes of scented, pastel cloth stirring softly from some unseen breeze.

Grump made us stop before going in. "My favorite room. It's just beautiful. Beautiful. And it has the most beautiful things inside. The best ever. Everyone says so. Everyone. There's more treasure here than anywhere."

Noticing the lack of guards, I asked, "Then, why no armed men?"

He smirked. "The GOP Room is free to use. You can help yourself at any time. Any time."

"GOP Room?" I asked. It seemed odd that a term from the United Colonies was employed here. I imagined former senators and congressmen assembling, but I began to hear feminine giggles from within as I brushed aside a stripe.

"You know what GOP stands for?" he asked.

"Sure. Grand Old Party."

His smirk grew.

We stopped inside the room. More divans, throw pillows, beds, and hot tubs filled the octagonal space, colorful light from stained glass windows splashing across it all. In the sunbeams, sweet-smelling white smoke that I recognized as marijuana curled and drifted on a soft breeze from an open window. On gilded tables spread about the room stood decanters of Grump wine, cheese, crackers, caviar, bread, fruits, veggies, bowls of dipping sauce, and colorful pastries. On one wall hung a variety of whips, chains, and restraints. A wardrobe full of costumes like a French maid or dominatrix beckoned the eye. In the corner sat a nude trio of women playing Bach on string instruments. Another step inside would've carried me from the tile floors onto a thick, golden carpet emblazoned, like everything, with a giant "T."

But what most caught the eye was the female flesh proudly on display for us. With heaving bosoms and sultry lips, dozens of scantily clad or nude females lounged in seductive poses. They were Asian, negro, and Latino, with only a few white women. Each wore rouge on her cheeks. Eyelashes had been teased to perfection. Long hair predominated, whether worn tightly, free or in exotic styles; one even wore them like Princess Leia from *Star Wars: A New Hope* and had donned an appropriate white, nearly see-through dress, with no bra (because those don't exist in space).

On seeing us, the women turned around as one and presented their nude backsides to us. Then, in unison, they said, "Grab our pussies!"

Grump beamed at me. "I never get tired of that. Never."

"A harem," I remarked in realization. That's what a GOP Room was.

"One of several. This one is the best. The best. It's good to be the emperor."

"I notice few of the women are white."

"Yes, of course. White women are free citizens and to be treated with respect. Well, some anyway. Can't get too carried away with that. They start demanding things. Gotta keep 'em in line. A good smack always does the trick. But the rest are slaves by law and common knowledge."

"Are the white women here different?"

Chapter 3 – "The GOP Room"

Grump jabbed me with an elbow as we looked at the girls in his harem. "Why do you think the white women are here? They're hoping I might use them. What a great honor! I rarely grant it, but my sons and others in the Inner Party are in here all the time. All the time. The other whites are captured liberals; we use them for really rough sex. You know the kind I mean."

"Yes, of course, sir." I had never believed all the liberal complaints about Grump's misogyny, but it was hard to ignore, standing there with sex slaves before us. I had already noted one white woman with a black eye and now understood. "So, you mean the other white women come here voluntarily hoping to, uh, have sex with you? Why aren't there more, then?"

"We have a lottery system to keep the numbers down. The white women can all get pregnant, by the way. In fact, we insist on being fertile. Gotta spread the master race genes, especially mine. They're the best. The best. But the others have been neutered."

I knew better than to correct him, as that was the term for removing a male's reproductive organs and spayed was the term for doing the same to females. "So, the minority women, they cannot have children. Very wise."

"Of course. I'm a genius. A very stable one. We can't have them reproducing at all, not to mention with royal blood. We're trying to wipe them out. Fix God's mistake. We're gonna take over their shit hole countries before we're through."

After a moment, I saw a familiar figure in the corner. A nude Ted Spoogent lounged between two beauties, who were stroking his shriveled manhood as he leered around the joint between his lips. On seeing me, Ted nodded a greeting.

"Try the food," suggested the emperor. "It's the best." He picked up a pastry and held it one way. "See, it forms a T upside down, but turn it over..." He did so and it formed an erect penis with two testicles, a design that could not be missed, given the artful hair carved into the balls and the circumcised head at the other end.

Not wishing to offend, I took the offered pastry, wondering what to bite off first. I opted for one testicle, then the other. I dared not put both in at once for fear of appearing greedy. And as I put the head into my mouth, feeling an odd rush of pleasure I hadn't expected, Grump beamed at me.

"They're all drugged, by the way."

"I'm sorry?" I tried to ask this around a mouthful of baked genitalia. Only now did I notice that each cupcake was a breast with a proud nipple straining upward. Each dipping sauce lay in a vulva-shaped container and the veggies and crackers had all been fashioned into either tongues or a penis.

"Marijuana. Some other stuff. Dr. Karson cooked up the recipe. You know I beat Hillary by fifty points."

I swallowed the rest of the penis, already starting to feel the effects of the drugs. I reached for another, bigger cock. "It was a great victory. Bigly. May I ask, what does Queen Telania think of this harem?"

"Ask her yourself, comrade," he replied, gesturing to one corner, and for the first time, I noticed the queen among the ladies. The cloud of marijuana smoke around her had obscured my vision, as had the multiple nubile girls who lay beside her, some fanning her and another feeding her grapes. Her gaze was dreamy, smug, and satisfied. I had decided not to ask her when she spoke up.

"I don't really care, do you?" the queen asked. Then she spread her legs and I averted my gaze. Well, after a quick peek.

"If you drop by at the right time," Grump added, "you'll find Ivanaka in here as well."

Startled, I inquired, "Surely not, uh, grabbing pussies?"

"No, no. We don't like lesbians here. Hunt them on the Safari. Any girl who enters a GOP room knows what's coming if a man walks in."

Speechless, I gazed about the room before finally asking, "Prince Jaryd doesn't mind?"

"It was his idea. She can be rather demanding, if you take my meaning. He's in here all the time anyway. Guy's got an appetite almost as big as mine! Bigly, I'd say. Very bigly. Speaking of appetites, looks like the drugs are working on you already." He poked my crotch and there, to my surprise, was an erection I hadn't noticed.

I stammered in embarrassment, but Grump just clapped his hands and several wenches rushed forward, pulling me toward a bubbling hot tub as they ripped off my clothes. I sensed that I had to please the emperor. He and Ted watched for what seemed like a long time as the women had their way with me and I felt no embarrassment in my drugged state, though this was quite unlike me. I felt free and euphoric. The emperor waved cheerfully and departed. I dare not describe the debauchery that followed.

I was ready for a second round of enjoying myself when a grinning Svetlana intervened, saying we had a busy day ahead and I'd have to revisit the GOP Room later if so inclined. She offered herself as an alternative, which caused a look of desire I failed to hide. She smirked and gave a running commentary on my merits as she redressed me like I was a schoolboy. The experience wasn't without its merits. Then she led me on a tour of the palace and grounds.

The latter didn't include the indoor GOP Grotto, which was reminiscent of the famed Playboy Mansion back in the U.C. The climate made it too cold for this outside, where manicured hedges had been carved into likenesses of Grump, flowers everywhere. Golden statues of His Majesty stood in many places, often alone but other times with others depicting men or women showing him deference and subservience. At times he was seen defending them from a beast of some kind, standing brave and gallant while other statues were fearful and cowed. Sometimes he rode a horse, bull, or even a dragon. A few fountains featured him as either a cherub or virile man, often nude and with large genitals that participated in the spraying of water or, in one case, champagne. All were larger than life. There could be no doubt what land you stood on.

The palace itself was enormous, with multiple wings of five to ten stories, branching out in a giant T shape (for "Grump"); I wondered if this was also shaped like a penis and balls as seen from above. The place was so big that she couldn't show it all and instead focused on what His Majesty most wanted... to impress me. We saw a grand ballroom, bowling alley, swimming pools, movie theaters and more. But the royal areas topped all others for sheer extravagance, mostly for the jewels, chandeliers, parquet floors, brocade and velvet curtains, and gold.

The main rooms of the royal family were even more ostentatious. Gems sparkled from nearly everywhere the eye fell.

Ornate pictures of the emperor and his family adorned the walls, some showing scenes of them hunting peculiar animals, the likes of which I'd never seen. Many were misshapen or appeared to be a fanciful cross between man and beast. The hunters sometimes held guns, as expected, but others were depicted holding gadgets whose purpose I could not fathom. I meant to inquire about them when my guide ushered me into Ivanaka's wing of the palace. We were apparently about to miss a weekly event of some kind.

As we approached a room at the end of a hall, its door stood open and a maid busied herself near a marble hearth. Hearing us coming, she quickly approached a nude statue of a child and yanked furiously on its erect penis. An opening in the wall beside her swung closed. Seeing her hastily look in our direction, I pretended I hadn't noticed as we continued around a corner.

We soon arrived at an octagon-shaped room where a crystal bathtub sat in the center. Above it hung a steel frame shaped like a cross, with manacles on each end. On the far wall, beneath stained-glass windows the color of blood, stood a dozen trembling girls, each stripped bare. All were Asian and fully grown, yet still in their teens. Princess Ivanaka stood before them in a silk bathrobe, her back turned to us. Several other women, obviously guards, held batons that had clearly been used more than once, based on the red welts seen upon several of the girls.

Hearing us enter, Ivanaka favored us with a glance before turning back to the girls. "Which of you would like to volunteer?" she asked them.

The girls glanced nervously at each other, but no one stepped forward.

"I promise it won't be painful if you do. Of course, I cannot give you a sedative, for that would alter the result. You understand."

Some of the girls nodded mutely. One appeared especially wide-eyed and began to pee herself, causing Ivanaka to nod at one of the guards, who slammed the baton across the girl's stomach. She doubled over and Ivanaka turned toward the tub and us. The guards roughly grabbed the chosen girl and hauled down the cross, quickly fastening the girl to it with the manacles. The device was re-hoisted above the bathtub, where Ivanaka stood, dropping her robe to the floor. She stood shameless before us, fully nude, and winked at me as she climbed in. Her father was right – Ivanaka had a beautiful body and, like him, I wanted her.

One of the guards used a spear to expertly slice open the chosen girl's neck and several arteries. I stifled a gasp. Blood began to flow down her, into the tub, and onto the princess, who closed her eyes, lay back, and smiled serenely as the tub began to fill drip by drip. Above her, the chosen girl slowly quieted and stopped writhing as her lifeblood drained. I struggled to control my expression lest I show disapproval.

We watched silently, no one moving. The guards were impassive. The remaining girls stood mute and frozen with horror, eyes far away. I suspected some had gone mad with fear or nearly so, but I sensed they knew better than to move, cry out, or otherwise draw attention to themselves. When the chosen girl stopped dripping, the cross was lowered, and her carcass was unceremoniously tossed aside. A guard chose another girl, seemingly at random, and brought her forward without resistance, like a lamb to the slaughter, one that had resigned itself unto death and knew no escape existed. On glancing at the tub, I saw that the blood in it only half-covered Ivanaka and she, therefore, needed more to fully submerge, if that was her goal.

Svetlana touched my arm and indicated it was time to leave. It was just as well. I didn't want to see anymore. The sound of the cross being hoisted once more was the last thing I heard before the doors closed behind us.

"What was that about?" I asked, feeling nauseous.

"She takes a weekly bath in the blood of virgin girls. It keeps her own skin young and supple."

I had no response. Barely hours into my visit, I already felt I had set foot in a madhouse. How was I last to last two weeks here? I already wanted to leave and never return. I'd want to forget but knew I never would. I'd never seen a dead body before and already so many had been killed in front of me. Did life have no value here? How could it after seeing this? And that interview with Grump, which Kellianne had mercifully cut short. There was an old idea that the attitude comes from the top, and if true, then the insanity was Grump's.

Lost in thought and muted distress, I listened quietly as Svetlana told me about other sights we passed, which included a food court. I noticed several seemingly familiar businesses that bore names I did not expect. A fast food place had a red and yellow logo of the word "McGrump". A chicken place looked just like KFC but had the letters TFC instead. Grumpcast was the lone provider of telephone and cable service. The list went on and on. Seeing my inquisitive look, Svetlana explained to me that, as part of the world's plot to "get" Grump, no foreign businesses would operate in Grumpland, so he'd been forced to steal their recipes or services and simply build similar but renamed – and vastly improved – businesses to suit his needs and those of his people.

"Everyone says they're much better," she concluded. "Everyone. You should try them."

"I will."

"When His Majesty is done conquering the world, he'll just replace those inferior brands with his own. The world will thank him. He's a very stable genius."

"That becomes harder to deny the more I see." Neither stable nor genius seemed to apply to him or anyone else here.

As we walked, I saw a sign for the National Gun Association that read, *NGA. Because that's who we shoot.* "What's that mean?" I asked.

She hooked one arm with mine. "How would you pronounce NGA?" she asked, spelling it.

I tried sounding out a few options in my head before saying in surprised realization, "Nigga."

Svetlana started laughing. "Wonderful slogan isn't it? Grump truly is a genius. He knew people would love it even if it's not entirely true. After all, we shoot gays, Muslims, and Mexicans, too. And Vikings. Liberals, of course. But it's a great slogan. One of the best. Everyone says so."

I feigned a smile of agreement. I knew racism existed everywhere and that various things said by the Republican party under Grump had been called racist by Democrats, but I'd been among those denying the comments were racist. Once again, I found that what had once been subtle was now overt and felt like a fool that I'd ever discounted the comments. Had the liberals been right? Even I could not doubt what I'd just discovered.

We continued our tour, with her leading me to lower levels. I'd been wondering where the captives were held, for it didn't seem like a prison or even a jail would exist. Grump just killed people on the spot. I suspected that anyone with the right to do so followed suit, which was seemingly anyone in the Inner Party, who likely gave orders to those in the Outer Party whom they tasked with doing it. Svetlana admitted that there were no judges, trials, or laws. But people *were* tortured. As a result, the prisoners were being kept below the palace in a dank, foul-smelling basement, where dried blood stained the sticky floor and walls in a large room with torture devices of every kind everywhere the eye fell. Many were situated above a drain. Two of them held malnourished victims who were currently getting a reprieve, while a corpse lay on another and a skeleton remained chained to one wall. A sign around its neck read, "Traitor!"

What surprised me most was the viewing area above one wall and a concert stage across from that. Svetlana revealed that Grump and others often gathered to watch the festivities while enjoying a banquet and concert to accompany the screams of the victims. A comic provided a running commentary and often interviewed both guests and the tortured, sometimes asking the former for suggestions on what to do next. She didn't know if either of the pilots were to be tortured and we didn't go to their cells, as the guards shooed us away.

Svetlana intended to show me more of the palace and grounds, but we received word that a new Golden Cruise had arrived, as the emperor had predicted that morning. A bustle of activity followed this announcement. I'd seen preparations being made all day, but it kicked up a notch as thousands of people were to be bussed to Grump Square. I spent the next hour walking around outside with Svetlana and learning details of the palace's exterior, the guard and their functions, and how the ceremony was to take place. Meanwhile, busses continually arrived in two locations, one depositing arrivals into Grump Square and others unloading them in an area behind the stage. I noticed that the former were predominantly males and dressed in whatever clothes they'd arrived in. The latter were all females, all of them lovely and wearing high heels and thick, white robes.

"His Majesty likes to welcome the women personally," Svetlana advised me. "The men will see how this unfolds, and you can see a select group of existing citizens arriving on foot from the town below. They have a role to play in demonstrating for the arrivals how people are expected to behave. You will see what I mean."

In the next hour, everyone assumed their places, the crowd calmed, and an air of quiet excitement grew. The new arrivals were near the stage and mixed in with existing citizens, who could be identified by wearing a virtually identical, grey, one-piece outfit with long sleeves, pants, a hood, and no pockets. The nobility sat on golden bleachers at the stage's rear, where my handler and I were given honorary seats among them. Various slave-girl servants provided refreshments to those of us on the stage before moving to stand quietly to one side, behind a barricade that would prevent the crowd from seeing them. They were dressed much the same as the proles, except with short sleeves and pants, and a steel collar around their necks.

At last, the arrival of Sean Spacer indicated the ceremony was to begin. He began by announcing and welcoming everyone. Then a majestic brass fanfare performed a piece called the Grump Promenade, during which His Majesty slowly strode from the palace, across a red-carpet lined bridge, and onto the stage, as everyone rose, clapped, and the crowd went wild. The cheering outlasted the music and Grump stood at a podium, grinning broadly and waving, basking in the adulation. He finally motioned for everyone to be quiet.

"My great people," he began, "you're truly great and getting greater all the time. And here we are with thousands of new citizens to welcome to this great empire of mine."

Not for the first time, I couldn't help thinking this was a kingdom, not an empire. The latter requires him to control more than his own sovereign power, but he didn't. He was a king, not an emperor.

"Before we get too far," he continued, "it's time for a song. I think you know the one I mean." Loud laughter greeted this. "Everyone know what time it is?" Grump asked the crowd. And they roared, for they'd seen Ted Spoogent behind him on the stage, strutting around with nothing on but a loincloth and a guitar, his leathery, sagging skin a sight to behold. "It's time for our favorite song, the Grump National Anthem! What's it called?"

Those in the crowd who were already proles roared, "Grab 'Em By the Pussy!"

"It's called what?" Grump repeated, grinning.

"Grab 'Em By the Pussy!" The new citizens joined in this time.

He asked again and they obliged him once more.

"Ted!"

Chapter 4 – "A Golden Welcome"

As Grump moved aside, the band roared into a rollicking up-tempo rocker that oozed sex appeal and lust. Ted sashayed around the stage, licking his lips and gyrating his hips in ways that came across differently than he might've thought at his advanced age. A line of the white-robed women, about to become citizens, was ushered onto the stage behind him, most looking confused, apprehensive, or a little excited. A guard made them turn their backs to the crowd before he ordered them to drop the robes to their feet. They exchanged concerned looks, none of them complying. This appeared to be expected, for a half dozen guards stormed the stage and violently ripped the robes from them, leaving them bare except for the white high heels. The cool afternoon air couldn't have felt comfortable but was no doubt anything compared to be stripped naked before lust-filled men. The guards forced them to bend over with their hands on their knees, their butts aimed at the cheering crowd, who saw their private parts with ease. A few of the women were already crying, but most appeared frozen, not from the cold, but with horror.

The band had been repeating the same section of music again and again before starting a verse, where Ted sang, "Grabbed her by the pussy and she purred my name. Grabbing by the tits, just ain't the same. Bent her over and took what I needed. Didn't even slow me when she started to bleed."

As looks of shock appeared on the women's face, Ted started the chorus by shouting, "Grab 'em!"

And the crowd echoed him. "Grab 'em!"

"Grab 'em!" from Ted.

"Grab 'em!" from the crowd.

"Grab 'em!" from Ted.

"Grab 'em!" from the crowd.

"By the pussy!"

He and the crowd repeated this three more times. Then Ted bounced around the stage before the next verse, which went, "The night is young and I'm ready for more. Girls everywhere, all of them whores. They want my man meat, it's ready to go, yeah. Gonna shove it, right into this ho, yeah." Another chorus followed this, and by now several women were crying, tears pouring down their faces. A few others were smiling, and one or two were into the show, rhythmically bouncing their rears to the tune and causing shouts of approval and a few men to point at them and clap.

Ted let out a yell and did a solo that consisted mostly of him yanking on the guitar's whammy bar suggestively before a final chorus. The song ended with a roar of approval from the crowd. They started to chant his name, and for a moment, he relished it. But then his gaze fell on His Majesty looking increasingly vexed. Ted turned white and ran to the nearest microphone, repeatedly yelling "Grump" instead of "Ted." Fortunately for him, the crowd took his cue and followed suit. He looked at Grump, who nodded approval and began to smile. On shaking legs, Ted stepped back.

Grump strolled to the first woman, who stood on trembling legs, and expertly shoved his fingers into her vagina as her face turned crimson. He felt around a little, then pulled his hand back and sniffed it, making a show of seeming pleased. He smacked her ass and then walked to the next one and did the same without having cleaned off his hand. Down the line he went, alternating between expressions of amusement, approval, or outright lust. Sometimes he felt their breasts, squeezing nipples, and even mimed fucking them from behind to laughter.

When he finished with these women, they were escorted from the stage and another line of them was brought up for the same treatment. Three more times he did this, with Svetlana telling me that only the most beautiful new citizens, always blondes, were officially greeted personally this way, with a lucky few selected for the GOP Room the very first night. These were usually the ones who appeared to enjoy it the most, as the others would need time to learn their proper place here in Grumpland. However, as all new arrivals witnessed the event, it was easy to believe that all of them understood the paradigm shift into which they'd entered.

Grump nodded at Ted, who ran up to the microphone and yelled, "Inspection time!" It was the title of another hit song they kicked off, this one about an immigration examination with a lustful ending. One final girl had been left dancing nude on the stage beside him, for she was the most eager to please. And when the song was over, he dropped his guitar and threw her over one shoulder, carrying her off to cheers.

His Majesty stepped up to the microphone. "Always a wonderful performance from our Minister of Music. He's a great patriot. A great patriot." He paused for applause and then added, "We have a very special guest with us here today, all the way from the Treasonous United Colonies."

"Hail Grump!" the cried roared in perfect unison before falling silent.

"Never get tired of that. Never," he mused. Then he bid me to step up to him. I bowed upon arriving. "This is Max. He's a great friend to our nation. A great friend." The crowd cheered me, waving. "He tells the one and only truth about us here in Grumpland to those back in the Treasonous United Colonies."

"Hail Grump!"

"Many of you know him, right? You saw him on TV back there. He's the one who tells the world about our wonderful Golden Cruises. That's how all of you got here. Well, to honor him for all that's he's done, today I have made him a citizen!"

The crowd clapped and roared so loud that my hair blew back and a foul stench caught my nose. I nearly gagged, tears springing to my eyes. Fortunately, Grump didn't see the brief look of horror that crossed my face before I controlled it and smiled through the agony. He turned then and saw the tears fall down my grinning cheeks, causing him to beam in pleasure.

He said to the crowd, "Look at that. Overcome with pride. Wonderful! I knew his heart was always in the right place. Always. You know, I'm personally giving him a tour of the whole, wonderful country so that he can tell the world just how much better we have it here!"

The crowd cheered again until he quieted them.

"They should've listened to us, but no. No, they had to have it their way. I tried to tell them. I tried. The damn Dems just wouldn't listen. Ruined that country. It's a shit hole now. A shit hole, just like the rest of the world. Overrun with Mexican rapists, colored people, you name it. They just pour in through the borders, but not here, right? I'm protecting you from that, because we have the biggest, greatest wall ever built!"

The crowd roared and moved toward the stage so that the guards lining the front of it had to beat them back. Water cannons began spraying them in the frigid air, but none of them seemed to mind. They calmed and backed up, a few trampled underfoot and ignored. Grump stood grinning through it all.

"It's better than the Great Wall of China! Another shit hole country. This whole planet is a shit hole. That's why we're gonna leave it together one day, right?"

The crowd clapped and hollered agreement, many raising a red vial into the air from where it was tied around their necks with a leather cord. From a distance, I'd seen these on nearly everyone's neck but my own and Svetlana's, though a few wore them in other places like their wrist. I'd had been wondering what they were for.

"The time is coming soon," Grump continued, "I promise you. I promise. I never lie. I'd never lie to you. Everyone else does, but not me. The fake news can't get you here. Not anymore. I keep it out. That's why there's only one TV channel here, and it's one I control. I alone. The Real News Network is my baby. Only I can fix everything, and only I am telling you the truth. Most of you haven't seen Max since you arrived here because only I can see his reports from the Treasonous United Colonies."

"Hail Grump!"

"Max can come with us now, isn't that right, comrades?"

They cheered.

"Everyone has their Special Grump Wine at the ready?"

Every person who hadn't already done so, even the children, lifted their vial aloft. The Inner Party members on the stage behind us did so. Grump had one, too. Only the new arrivals, Svetlana, myself, and the slaves did not.

"Great. Great. You're all great citizens. Don't worry, Max. We'll get you one, too. When I give the signal on the Foretold Day, we'll all drink it and pass on from this world to the next. This Earth isn't good enough for us, the master race!"

More loud cheering filled the air and a few people standing amidst the new arrivals got so carried away that they emptied their vials down their throats. At once they fell, convulsing as a red froth gushed from their peeled back lips and they clawed at the air. In a few moments, they lay lifeless as the existing citizens around them hooted and hollered and the new arrivals stared uncomprehendingly. For the first time, I heard Grump laugh, a sinister mix of callousness, condescension, and unhinged self-adulation.

I tried to avoid looking aghast. They had gone mad. All of them. From the self-indulgent Inner Party right down to the lowest proletariat. I had been sending people to this evil place, not knowing what awaited them. Had they? No. No, they couldn't have. Grumpland was the most secretive place on Earth, even more so than North Korea. And it was no wonder. How could they have known? How long did it take for new arrivals to become indoctrinated in a mindset that caused this? I shuddered, my eyes on those golden cruisers who stood nearest. Some of their faces were white, while others looked up at His Majesty with awe, a slow smile of wonder spreading across their lips. Now I understood why a few people killed themselves at the rally. I suspected it was no accident, that they had been selected and strategically placed to both get a point across about the expected level of submission, and to inspire that very thing. It was long known to humanity that those willing to die for a mission, a man, or a madness would inspire others to do the same.

Grump said, "Alright, alright. Everyone just calm down. I love the show of devotion. I really do. You guys are the best ever. Everyone says so. But I need you to remain alive until I give the signal, okay? Can you do that for me?" They loudly agreed until he waved them down again. "You know, I had a great meeting with Satan the other day. And you know what he said? He said, sir, sir, you're doing a wonderful job here. I'm so proud of you and your people."

The crowd roared.

"You know, some people might find it distasteful that I had to make a deal with the devil, but that's what you have to do when the Treasonous United Colonies is out to get you."

"Hail Grump!"

"I would've made you all rich by now but there's a conspiracy aimed at stealing our money. The Dems are the ones behind it. It's another hoax, another witch hunt for illegal funds or something stupid. They're just jealous. The reality is that I'm kicking their ass. You'll all be very rich soon and dressed just like the Inner Party up here with me."

More cheering.

"I have an important announcement. It's bigly. Very bigly. This is the gift I'm giving to all of you. You might even say it's because we don't have that money for you yet. But you know? This gift is worth far more. It's invaluable. You ready'?" He paused as they cheered. He asked again, working up the crowd, then a third time. He finally seemed satisfied. "Okay. Okay, here it is. You're gonna love this. Everyone says so. Everyone.

As of today, all firstborn males in Grumpland are to be named Donald, after me, the greatest man who's ever lived. Isn't that great?"

Wild applause met this. I saw multiple men with tears of joy pouring down their faces, their wives hugging them. A few seemed humbled and grateful while others were downright horny, starting to have sex right there on the cold stone pavers, the women around them rooting on the men and their proud erections.

Grump gazed at one of the nearest couples for several minutes before adding, "It's retroactive, too. So, all of you firstborns are now called Donald. Don't call your firstborn son by anything else or you know what happens."

The crowd laughed and Grump gestured off to one side, where a curtain rose to reveal Stephen Killer, Grump's lead on immigration policy back when Grump was still President of the United Colonies. He wore a black executioner's cape and maniacal grin as he swung a sword with great force at a black slave tied to a rack. The blade decapitated him, the head rolling across the stage and splattering blood everywhere. Then Killer cut off both arms and legs, ripped open his stomach to spread the entrails around, and set him on fire. While the body burned, he pulled out stick with a marshmallow on it and began toasting it. Only now did I spy the bag from which they'd come, right beside a box of graham crackers and some chocolate bars.

As I looked away, my gaze met that of a slave girl with a golden nose ring and skin blacker than any I'd ever seen. Her piercing brown eyes held mine as if meaning to impart an understanding of something on her mind, but I did not understand. She looked away, but moments later glanced back before studiously avoiding my eyes as I continued to watch her on and off.

His Majesty sat on his throne as a military parade began, with soldiers, tanks, and other equipment moving menacingly into the crowd, which had to quickly move out of the way to avoid being crushed. Not everyone made it, several bodies visible after the first vehicle went by, just before the second mashed it even more. Those nearby laughed and pointed.

"Gotta be faster than that," Grump joked to no one in particular. "We only accept the elite here. Slowpokes get what they deserve."

I nodded to him in fake agreement as helicopters, bombers, and fighters flew overhead, performing elaborate moves meant to impress us. All the while, patriotic sounding music played through loudspeakers. I quickly grew weary of the spectacle but Grump, who apparently saw this regularly, appeared to enjoy every moment of it. I felt relieved when it finally ended. This was usually how this affair resolved, but Grump had something special planned.

"Those sacrifices you saw earlier," Svetlana began quietly, "when people drank their vials, they were chosen based on essays they had written to His Majesty, who never reads them, of course. Others make the choice on his behalf."

"What do the essays say?"

"People must convince us they're worthy to make the sacrifice."

"By saying what?"

She squeezed my thigh playfully. "Wouldn't you like to know? I'm kidding. Don't look so upset. No one knows what the winning essays say so that no one can cheat. Authenticity of devotion is important."

I nodded. "How many people write one?"

"Oh, everyone but the slaves, who are unworthy, of course. Even the children. It's important."

My eyes went to the slave girl with jet black skin, finding her watching me until our eyes met. "Surely not the children who aren't old enough to write?"

"Those kids are interviewed, and their thoughts are written down for them."

"What about the kids who can't talk yet?"

"They're shown a picture of His Majesty and the purity of their resulting smiles is photographed. If these are deemed sufficient, they can be chosen."

I felt momentarily disoriented by the idea of this being done to babies, as if my morality had just violently clashed with theirs and I couldn't process what I'd just heard. They had apparently thought of everything. "But they're too young to take the potion."

She rolled her eyes. "It's mixed into their baby formula or milk, silly."

Again, I felt dizzy. "And their own parents administer the dose?"

"With pride."

"How many infants or toddlers have been sacrificed this way?"

"Not many. Just a few dozen over the last ten years."

The matter-of-factness of the statements added to the cruelty. It was almost as if she wasn't even human. "So, about three a year?"

"Give or take. It's too bad none were chosen for today, so you could've seen it. They don't convulse like the adults. They just get this adorable look of surprise. It's more peaceful. Kind of beautiful, really. Maybe I'll have one do it for you."

I blanched. "No, it's okay. I'll take your word for it. Maybe next time."

"Suit yourself."

While we'd been talking, the audience crowded around the stage, as they'd been told that an additional announcement was coming. I made eye contact with the jet-black slave once more.

Grump began, "I have a special treat for all of you. You're not gonna believe this, but it's true. I swear it's true. We don't do fake news here. Earlier today, my elite forces shot down a fighter plane. You'll never guess where it's from."

People began shouting guesses, with most of them being right. Finally, Grump told them.

"The Treasonous United Colonies!"

"Hail Grump!"

"That's right. They're planning an attack, just like I told you they would. But you saw all those tanks and planes we got just now. We're gonna bomb the shit out of them soon, that I promise you."

A big cheer met this.

"But there's an even bigger surprise. We captured not one, but two of the pilots on that plane."

The crowd went wild.

"They're both Democrats!"

I didn't think the mob could get any louder, but they did.

"Do you want to see them?" He paused as they roared. He asked a few more times, always waiting as their volume rose even higher. Finally, he made a gesture and two racks on wheels rolled onto the stage. We got our first look at the captives, who were chained to the steel so that their legs were spread, and their arms were above their heads. The black man was tall with a shaved head and didn't appear to have been modified in any way, but the blonde woman had clearly had makeup applied to her face. Garish red lips, long lashes, and pink cheekbones made her look like a cheap whore. She'd been dressed like one, too, in a flimsy negligee that did little to hide her feminine charms, her long hair pulled over one shoulder. Grump let the crowd yell and throw food at the prisoners for a few minutes before quieting them.

"Can you believe she was wearing this under her uniform?" he asked. Boos. "What a slut." More boos. "Maybe I should inspect her?" A chorus of denials flowed. "She doesn't deserve the honor, does she?" Loud agreement. "I'll tell you my plans for her in a minute. But first, you'll never guess what we're doing to do with this guy. You know what his name is? Barry. I wonder who else went by that. I forget. Let me think. Oh wait, I think it's coming to me. Yeah, yeah. I think it was the guy who was President of the Treasonous United Colonies before me."

"Hail Grump!"

"That's right. It was Barak Osama." Loud booing interrupted him about the previous President of the United Colonies. "You know he was a Muslim, right? He wasn't even born in the country. It was some shit hole country in Africa. That's what I heard. Everyone knows it, too. Everyone. Never should've been allowed to be president. It was treason."

By this point, the wild cheering was so loud that he paused to either bask in it or let it die down. I couldn't tell which. The jet-black slave looked away shyly when our eyes met again.

"You know what we should've done with good ol' Barry, right? Well, we're gonna do it to this one. We're gonna hunt him on the Safari!"

The crowd went nuts.

"And you know I always share these hunts with you, so you're gonna get to see the whole thing live on Grump TV!"

Someone in the crowd was so overcome that she fainted. Two of the nearby men began groping her while others cheered them on. Grump watched in amusement.

"That's right, boys. Let her have it. She wants it. You can tell. She's not even resisting. Me, I like some fight left in them, you know? Makes it more fun. Just kiss her. Don't even wait. When you're emperor, you can do whatever you want. They let you do it. You guys need a Tic Tac?" He watched for a few more minutes until speaking up again, grinning.

"You know, I forgot to mention something about this whore co-pilot up here. You'll never guess what her name is. It's Hillary!" The crowd lost their shit. "I'm serious. You guys are probably thinking I'm making this up, but I'm not. And you know her last name? It's Delosi. She's actually a relative of Nasty Nancy. You remember Nasty Nancy, right? She's the one who tried to impeach me."

Wild boos ensued for the former Speaker of the House back in the United Colonies, one of Grump's favorite enemies.

"It was a witch hunt. Presidential harassment. No one has ever been treated so poorly as me. It was terrible. Terrible. Everyone says so. But listen, this week we have our great Hillary

Fest, and you know this is always the best time. The best. But this time it's gonna be even better because I've made a very special decision. You're gonna love it. Everyone says so. Everyone. We're going to put Crooked Hillary Delosi into the Wicker Hillary and burn her alive as a sacrifice!"

A deafening roar erupted from the crowd. Grump seemed to decide nothing else would top that and waved before leaving the stage. The rest of us began to follow, heading back to the palace as the crowd chanted his name long after we were inside. He sometimes stopped to shake hands with fawning sycophants so that Svetlana and I caught up with him.

"You'll join me on the Safari?" Grump asked, and I knew it to not be a question, though the thought of watching a man be hunted for sport already sickened me.

"I would be honored, sire."

"You're a hunter, right? Maybe I'll let you have a crack at him."

"Again, you're too kind, Your Majesty."

"You won't think that when I'm shooting at him." He barked out a laugh. "First, I'll have Svetlana give you an island tour. You can see the wicker woman we'll be putting Hillary inside. You know I beat her by seventy-five points?"

"It was a great victory."

He clapped me on the back and went elsewhere, disappearing into a throng of admirers among the Inner Party. I felt relieved to be rid of him for now, sick as I already was at this land he'd created with my help. Svetlana took me by the hand and led me away inside the palace.

She smiled at me. "I saw you looking at the Ebony Girl. I think she likes you."

Chapter 5 – "A Night to Remember"

I arched an eyebrow. "Ebony Girl? Who's that?"

Svetlana replied, "The slave girl with the unusually dark skin. She's notorious for it. His Majesty singled her out for it and sometimes has her at important functions."

"Why?" I wondered if I had somehow jeopardized the girl with our eye contact.

"He doesn't say. Despite her inherent inferiority because she's black, there's something undeniably beautiful about her. I think he's intrigued by just how dark she is. I suspect he's hoping to find a white woman who has the same qualities." I had no comment on this, and after a moment she remarked, "You can bed her if you like. Do you want her sent to your chambers?"

"Uh, I, uh..."

She laughed. "You blush like a schoolboy, comrade. If you make up your mind, just tell any servant in the palace and they'll fetch her for you. She's known as Ebony Girl."

I nodded and changed the subject. "What's happens to everyone now?"

"They go to Central Processing," Svetlana answered. "We already know where the citizens will be placed. It depends on their skill sets and how much money they've brought with them. Most of them will join the proletariat or becomes proles as we call them. They live in government-furnished housing while we invest their savings for them so that they can one day become wealthy and join the Outer Party. Each of the males will be given a new name, typically Donald now, but sometimes

Eric or Barron, and they'll be given a haircut like His Majesty, to show devotion and solidarity with our great leader."

I had noticed all the combovers even from a distance. "What about the women? Do they get new names?"

She rolled her eyes. "Of course not. Females are only for breeding and sex, not necessarily in that order. They aren't worthy, but they sometimes adopt versions of Ivanaka or Telania on their own."

Hearing a woman say things made me too speechless to address it, but then Svetlana was a member of the Outer Party and a gift from Poohtin. She likely had special privileges and hadn't needed to worry about rising from the proletariat. "How often does that happen, joining the Outer Party?"

"So far, never, because there's a deep state conspiracy against His Majesty from the world's banks, so it's become difficult to enrich our citizens."

"That's unfortunate." I knew better than to ask for details on the conspiracy. I had repeated a few in my day, which was one reason I was taken aback by the number of them that had already come out of Grump's mouth just today. Had I sounded that crazy? Having not heard him repeat conspiracies in a decade, and those here growing extreme without the outside world hearing them, the bullshit nature of them had struck me like a blow from which I was still reeling. In Grump's world, no one ever explained or provided proof of such claims.

She continued, "Some of the wealthiest will become members of the Outer Party, which is about two percent of the population. They help run everything in Grumpland, doing the actual work except for the menial tasks the slaves must do."

"Do they also get new names and a haircut?"

"Yes. It's only the Inner Party that allows for individualism, where people keep their names and can adopt their own look, provided His Majesty approves, of course. The Inner Party is reserved for His Majesty and the nobles you met today. It's virtually impossible to attain membership there at this point, as one must do extraordinary service for His Majesty and the empire." She looked sideways at me. "You're one of the few who might have the chance, given the great work you've done telling those outside our world of how great it is to come and live here."

My stomach churned as I was only beginning to grapple with the reality that I had helped send these people to. "I would be honored, but I seek no appointments."

"That's one reason he's considering it. Your motives are pure."

Only now had we walked far enough into the palace for the chanting outside to fade. "What happens to the slaves now?"

"The slaves will be taken to their district and indoctrinated into their new lives. All will take a skills test to learn where they can best be used. Each will have a physical, and if deemed unworthy or otherwise useless, will be turned loose on Grump's Safari for hunting later."

I had to know. "They're hunted?"

She chuckled. "Yes, silly. For sport. It keeps the nobles happy to have fresh game for the hunt."

An impression now seemed more certain. "The Safari is a hunting ground."

"Yes. You'll have a chance to see it, I'm sure. As for the slaves, each will be given a brand to denote which district they belong to. The psychological effects of being branded are well known. They know that they are property and can be disposed of at will. It keeps them in line."

"I'm sure it does." Not looking appalled was becoming harder.

"It's important that we break their spirit, so there's a process we put them through to ensure this."

"I guess I don't really need details."

"Some of it is unpleasant, to be sure, but it's for the common good. You'll have a chance to see where they live soon, but you should rest a while before the banquet tonight."

With that, she escorted me to my rooms, but along the way, we stopped to talk with various sycophants. Most invited me to visit their own homes if time permitted, fawning over me with appeals to enjoy their own GOP Rooms or other delights, which they admitted couldn't compare with Grump's but were otherwise better than anyone else. I suddenly understood how pleasing it must've been for the emperor to have his ass kissed so frequently.

And yet I grew tired of it, and so Svetlana and I continued on our way, though more people stopped us to speak with me. It seemed like everyone wanted me to report on how wonderfully they were doing to those back in the states. They were also competing with each other rather shamelessly, almost arguing as they tried to one-up each other. But at last we broke away toward the royal suites, which my rooms were near. Once inside, I asked for some time alone and Svetlana kissed my cheek before leaving.

I spent an hour trying to clear my mind of everything I'd seen, disturbing ideas and images competing for the right to make me vomit into the toilet, right onto Hillary Minton's face. It seemed that everywhere I looked, racism, misogyny, and intolerance were championed. Like everyone back home, I'd known of Grump's tendencies in this regard, but somehow, I'd never really believed it. I'd told myself it was just a show. That the fake news was responsible for characterizing his words and actions. But there was no denying it here. It raged stronger and freer than I ever could've imagined. I wanted to get out of this place but had two weeks left before I could. I felt no self-pity, for my predicament paled in comparison to that of everyone on this island except for the Inner Party, with whom I was to dine before long.

Disturbed by the thought, I opened a bottle of chilled wine and poured a bigger glass than was wise, but I couldn't help it. I practically chugged it and poured myself another. I started to feel a buzz soon and realized that controlling my expressions might be harder if I became too inebriated, so I reluctantly stopped. But it achieved the desired effect and made me feel almost dismissive of the insanity I'd already witnessed. Perhaps it was all just a delusion from which I'd now woken and laughed off. Maybe if I kept this buzz going through dinner, I could laugh for real at the next atrocity brought before me.

Mercilessly, I had little time to myself, for my handler collected me once more and we set off. To indicate the esteem in which Emperor Grump held me, I'd been invited to meet him and the empress in their rooms prior to a banquet to be held in his honor. Svetlana and I passed other nobles along the way, some asking me to give their well wishes to Grump. Everyone seemed desperate to please him. Was the Inner Party living in terror, too?

We passed multiple guards in spotless uniforms as we entered a kind of inner sanctum, where the emperor and empress lived in luxury, the likes of which I'd never seen, even in photos of the wealthiest homes on Earth. I couldn't help thinking that all of the money the citizens brought was paying for this. Otherwise, it didn't make sense. If a deep state conspiracy was making it impossible to grow the wealth brought here, then it should've had the same effect on Grump's ability to gild himself so extravagantly. The money had to be coming from somewhere.

The emperor had an entire wing of his own, with much of it empty, and far into it was the suite of rooms where he actually lived. To my surprise, I was ushered into the sitting area just outside the bedroom. My host and his wife were bickering over just how much of their world I should be shown, but they stopped as we entered. Bidding to sit, His Majesty had us served wine and cheese as we spent a short while chatting about golf, during which he aired an old grievance, something about offshore windmills destroying a golf course he bought.

Suddenly Grump stood up, pressed his knees together tightly, and shoved his hands into his crotch. "I have to go potty!"

Empress Telania rolled her eyes at me and led her husband to the bathroom, went inside with him, and then returned a minute later, closing the door. We talked idly of minor things like how many joints she smoked in a day and whether Ted Spoogent was as bad in bed as she claimed, when we heard the emperor cry out excitedly. He called us to gather around, so we went to do the door, opened it, and found him standing there with his pants around his ankles. Seeing us, he pointed into the toilet, beaming with pride.

"Look what I made!"

With dread creeping over me, I gazed down and saw three, very tiny circles of poop atop the image of Hillary Minton painted there, as it was on all toilets throughout the realm.

"A doody! A doody! A doody!" he said happily, clapping his hands, now that he'd counted them.

"Should we call Guinness, sire?" Svetlana asked, pressing a speed dial button on her iGrump, a phone that looked and functioned exactly like an iPhone.

"Of course," replied Telania.

"You mean the world record people?" I asked.

Svetlana nodded. "Yes. He bought them last year. He now holds all the world records."

Grump grinned. "And now I'll hold this one, too! My poops are bigger than anyone's," he bragged. "Wanna know why?"

"Yes, my lord."

"Because I'm more full of shit than anyone!" he announced without a trace of irony.

He'd barely finished this statement when two men in white lab coats entered the room before scooping out the tiny poops. They murmured in excitement as they measured. For the first time, I noticed Grump's orange skin wasn't only his hands and face. And when he bent over to lift his pants, I learned more than I'd ever wanted. I excused myself to the other room and downed another full wine glass in one gulp, then decided I was done with that for the night.

The four of us soon left for dinner, where everyone else had already gathered. A string orchestra performed Mozart as we entered. Chandeliers were softly glowing above a table that must've been a hundred yards long, fine china, silver, crystal, and embroidered cloths adorning it all. Every twenty yards stood another giant meatloaf, Big McGrumps, fries, egg McGrumps, well-done steaks, chicken wings, taco bowls, and pizza. Servants stood by with decanters of Diet Grump and wine.

We received a standing ovation on entering and I learned my handler and I had been seated at a place of honor just below the royal family. I saw Ebony Girl standing near Grump's place, having been given the honor of serving him, as was often the case, I learned. She saw me and seemed visibly startled when our eyes met. After this, she avoided my gaze and I likewise tried not to dwell on her captivating presence for fear of drawing attention to her.

I expected a speech of some kind, but once we all sat, Grump picked up his soda and quickly addressed us. "To me, the greatest man who has ever lived."

"Hail Grump!"

Everyone drank. Then Grump grabbed a burger with one hand, some fries with another, and shoved both into his mouth. With this sign given, the slaves began serving food onto our plates. I glanced around as I tried to eat with some decorum, unlike most at the table, who talked with their mouths full, spilled food and drink on themselves, the table, and the floor, and sometimes spit some food over their shoulders at a servant upon deciding it wasn't warm or cold enough, or some other complaint. A few even threw food at the slaves and Ivanaka ordered one of them to be disciplined.

I assumed this would take place away from us, but the poor girl was stripped naked in one corner, beneath one of the enormous tapestries of Grump seducing women or slaying frightful animals that were straight out of someone's nightmare. The girl was whipped to the tune of the music playing. Only I and the other slaves seeming to notice or care. My eyes once again met those of Ebony Girl. She looked frightened and tense, sometimes subtly wincing at the whip's crack. She seemed to be trying to suppress any show of empathy, just as I was doing. I felt a look of shared horror pass between us before I wiped the look from my eyes and focused on a taco bowl before me.

Moments later, Donald Jr., who sat near me, swatted the air before him, suggesting a small insect was bothering him. Two slaves rushed forward, clapping their hands in the air near him as if to kill whatever it was. Jr. first seemed content that they were doing their jobs, but as time passed without a kill, he grew surly, sighed impatiently, snapped at them to do better, and finally clapped his own hands at the unseen nemesis again. This time he killed it and a smug smile of satisfaction grew as those in the room, who'd been watching, began to applaud with increasing fervor and shouts of "bravo!" As the slaves hurried away, he rose to his feet to bask in the glory, condescension and superiority oozing from him.

"What a man!" crowed Nic Hailey.

"Incredible!" shouted Jeweliani, not to be outdone.

"I've never seen anything like it!" Matt Gaytz beamed.

Then Randy Pawl began a chant that others took up. "Junior! Jun-ior! Jun-ior!"

This went on for several minutes, during which Jr.'s chest swelled with pride, he placed both hands on his hips, and he raised his chin into the air. I sensed he was holding back tears. For a moment, I thought he looked exactly like his father, only more snot-nosed and less orange. His wife leaned toward him and placed one hand on his clothed crotch, where an erection could barely be seen due to its unusually small size. I wondered if it, too, would die if someone clapped their hands together over it.

Finally, he sat down, dabbing at his eyes as the applause quieted.

"I've never been more proud," said his father.

"Incredible boy you've got there," Jeweliani interjected. "Incredible!"

Grump ignored him. "With such agility and great military leadership like yours to guide us, we will inevitably win any war with the Treasonous United Colonies."

"Hail Grump!"

Donald Jr. was their military leader? Didn't see that one coming. I also hadn't anticipated what happened next. Two slaves came forward, one holding a pair of tweezers, with which she picked up the dead insect and placed it on a small, golden plaque held by the other, quickly affixing it. The other slave bowed and humbly presented the trophy to the hunter who'd earned it. Jr. quickly passed it around the room, many nobles kissing the plaque before handing it to the next person. At my turn, I followed suit to avoid standing out, noticing that the bug was nothing more than a gnat. Written below it were the words, "Killed by Donald Jr." and the date.

Grump added, "Those amazing reflexes come from me, of course. I hereby grant you another title: 'Lightning Junior.'"

And now the tears flowed from Lightning Junior's face, which contorted as emotion overcame him and he sobbed like a child into a handkerchief. Amidst the great, wracking sobs, he sometimes raised his red face to gaze fondly at his father, to whom he declared, "I love you, dad!"

"Ted," began Grump, and Spoogent looked up from where he was masturbating at the table, pants around his ankles, "I want a new song performed at the next gathering. Call it 'Lightning Junior.' Make it the best song. The best song ever. In the olden days, musicians used to sing songs about great deeds like what we just saw. And, so will we. We'll make Grumpland ever greater."

Amidst the cheering, Ted raised one lubricant-covered hand to his forehead, saluting and inadvertently wiping some on his brow. "With the greatest pleasure, Your Majesty."

With a smirk, Grump asked, "Even more pleasurable than what you're doing now?"

"Of course, sire. Nothing pleases me more. I was performing my own salute to your magnificent son."

"Then continue, comrade."

"Thank you, Your Highness."

Most of us resumed dining, people conversing with Ted as if he wasn't jerking off in front of them. No one seemed to care. I got the impression this was fairly common. I had lost my appetite and instead sipped at the water, eager to be away from these people. Perhaps I could visit with the proles and learn more about their lives. I'd already had enough of the Inner Party and watched with envy as Jaryd excused himself and left. He'd hardly touched his food.

As often happens while eating with utensils, my knife and fork rubbed together, which is how I came to notice small flecks of gold coming off the fork. I discreetly peered at it and saw that it was cheap metal under the golden exterior. My eyes moved about the candelabras, serving dishes, and other gold items on display all around. Was everything fake?

As dinner concluded, the curtain pulled back to reveal someone from Guinness, who made a brief speech about how, just prior to the meal, the emperor had set a new record for size and volume of defecation. It was noted that his pellets were bigger than even that of a bull, that most virile of animals, to which His Majesty was deemed superior. His three poops from earlier were trotted out on a golden tray. Beside them were lifelike replicas of the previous record holding shit, which had also belonged to him. For comparison sake, a turd from several others were present as well, each smaller.

The assembled guests voted on to whom each piece of crap belonged, with mostly rightly guessing that Mike Pince had come in second place, Jeweliani third, and Billy Barre fourth. These individuals went to stand beside a beaming Grump, who was presented with a plaque for Bullshitter of the Month, a proud picture soon beamed to all in Grumpland via GrumpTV. Many aspired to one day become members of the Bullshitter of the Month club, but only members of the Inner Party could receive such recognition, though it didn't stop patriotic citizens from trying.

"Alright," began Grump, placing the poop-laden tray on a white pedestal, "we have a tasty dessert for most of you, but I want a show of loyalty and devotion. Who wants to eat my shit?"

Before he'd even finished speaking, Lindsey Gramm leapt up and was running as soon as his feet hit the ground. Ted Spoogent wasted precious seconds on a barbaric yell and yanking his pants the rest of the way off before his headlong pursuit, Devinn Noonez close behind. Ted caught Lindsey and wrestled him to the ground only to see Devinn go by them both, but Lindsey expertly tripped him. They tussled and tore at each other, knocking the poop from the pedestal. Ted was the first to grab a rolling piece of shit, trying to get it in his mouth, but Lindsey bit Ted's hand, and when he dropped the prize, it fell into Lindsey's eager mouth. He devoured it whole, then resumed beating the others with madness in his eyes. You wouldn't think a man in his 70s would have such vigor, but he easily overcame the other brownnosers. Soon another piece went down the hatch.

Without even looking, he kicked Ted where the sun doesn't shine and then began beating Devinn's head against the marble floor until blood spurt out and drenched the remaining crap. Lindsey picked it up and stood proud, exultant, as he raised it to his mouth. With a cackle of victory, in it went, and as he gulped it down, he triumphantly raised both brown-stained hands in the air, his shit-eating grin leaving no mystery as to what had gone down. Spoogent began wailing hideously, legs and feet kicking at the floor while he screamed and cried, tears and boogers pouring down his face. Grump stood beaming and waved at someone to clean them up. As slaves dragged Ted and the remains of Devinn away, Lindsey strutted all the way to his chair, tears of gratitude on his cheeks.

After order was restored, a teenage boy with Down Syndrome was shoved out onto a stage where the orchestra still sat, a speech in one of his hands. No sooner had he started talking than Grump began mocking him. Though the boy spoke well albeit slowly, Grump pretended he slurred words, mispronounced everything, and was generally dumb. Those at the tables loudly laughed, which only worsened when a man in a wheelchair was rolled out to also be mocked. He was followed by others with disabilities, whether mental or physical, until a half dozen of them shared the stage. Finally, the orchestra began playing "Putting on the Ritz" by Fred Astaire while they tried to sing along, which made the room descend into both cheers and boos, and started throwing cake, pie, and ice cream at them. At last it was over, and they were made to leave.

The court comedian took their place, stepping around the mess, her girth causing a few men to call her fat and ugly. Not until she spoke would I recognize former actress and stand-up comic Roseann Barre. Before she could say anything, Eric Grump decided to yell his own joke.

"How do you have sex with a fat pig like this one?" he asked. "Roll her around in flour and look for the wet spot!"

Everyone laughed, including Roseann. "Well I've got more than one wet spot for you, Your Highness, and you're welcome to them all!" This was met with applause and she dove right into her prepared jokes. "Ever wonder why the blacks are so skinny here in Grumpland? Because we don't have a KFC." The crowd chuckled as she pulled a chicken wing from a pocket and tossed it at one of the malnourished slaves, striking him in the face. The meat fell to the floor and he dutifully picked it up and tore into it with his teeth, to the delight of the nobles. I thought I saw his eyes water before he stifled the tears.

"Don't choke on that!" Roseann warned. "No one wants dinner ruined by watching you writhe around on the floor. No. Wait a minute. That would be funnier than that kid that was up here before." She waddled around the stage with exaggerated motions of incompetence, looking to the emperor for approval and getting two thumbs up.

"Alright," Roseann stated, "got a question for everyone. What do you get when two faggots have sex in the woods?" After a dramatic pause, she answered, "Kindling." Dead silence followed this joke and sweat broke out on her forehead. "Get it? A faggot is a bunch of little sticks. You know, like you'd use to start a fire, like kindling."

This produced a small chuckle. Grump frowned in disdain. Licking her lips nervously, eyes darting about the room, Roseann said, "Okay wait. I got a better one. What do you get when two Mexicans have sex in the rain? The beast with two wetbacks."

This produced a roar of approval and a standing ovation.

Grump stood grinning from ear to ear before announcing, "Well, it's not going to get any better than that. Thank you, Roseann."

She bowed and walked from the stage on shaking legs.

I couldn't take any more. To Svetlana, I quietly observed that I felt a little tired after my long day. She pouted that I was going to ruin her enjoyment of other festivities, but then agreed to take me back to my rooms, so we left with a nod of thanks and apology to His Majesty, who didn't seem at all bothered by my departure.

My suite was in sight when Svetlana and I heard a brief commotion, the sound of a physical struggle, a woman's protests, and finally a man's low murmur and a sigh of contented surrender. She shushed me as we approached a narrow hallway that led to the servant's quarters. A man with short black hair was bending a woman in a French maid's outfit with lace stockings and high heels over her laundry cart. Her long, black hair was thrown back along with her head, which tilted upward, her eyes half closed amid an expression of rapture. The man appeared to be kissing her neck. I heard a distinct slurping sound and wondered what juvenile was still interested in giving a hickey. But then the man turned and looked straight at us with bloodshot, glowing eyes, his lips stained with red that dripped down his chin, two sharp fangs protruding over them. I recognized Prince Jaryd with a start. Whether he recognized us or not, he turned back to the woman and resumed quenching his thirst. We walked away, to my relief.

As we reached the door to my rooms, I finally asked, "Is he...?"

She smirked. "A vampire? Of course, silly. Prince Jaryd has been one for ages. He prefers Jews and we keep a small supply of them here for him."

"Why?" I wasn't really sure I wanted the answer but had to know.

"They're cleaner."

"How so?"

"Well, they don't eat pork, for example, because pigs are dirty, so their blood is higher quality, more potent. And they don't breed with others as much, so the bloodline is purer. Besides, Jews have all the money and it's just a habit from his old life to prey on his own kind. You see, when he bites them, he controls them and their finances from there onward. That they no longer have money here in Grumpland doesn't matter. He just prefers it this way."

"I see. Are there other vampires here?"

"Oh yes. Some of us eat a dish with garlic in it for dinner every night to reduce our risk of becoming dinner ourselves." I searched my recollection of my meal to see if my selection had seemed garlicky. If so, it had been too subtle. On seeing my look, she laughed. "Don't worry. You're under His Majesty's protection. No one would dare. But if you step out of line..."

"I wouldn't dream of it." Truly, more peril existed at every moment here than I had imagined.

We arrived at my suite, which was unlocked, my bags nowhere in sight, though I saw that my laptop and a few other belongings had been removed from my luggage and sat on a table, charged and ready to use. I would soon discover that someone had bypassed all of the locks on my suitcases, opened each, and placed everything in drawers, on hangers in the walk-in closet, or put my toiletries in the bathroom. Whether this was more intrusive than helpful I didn't know, but my guard rose.

Partly for this reason, when Svetlana cozied up to me as if hoping to get an invitation to stay for carnal pleasures, I declined with some effort, eager to have some privacy, if that were possible. I suspected that cameras were everywhere, even in the bathroom, and that turning off the lights might also afford no discreetness, as the presence of infrared devices hardly seemed beyond Grump. Was my room bugged? Had a tracking device been put in or on my clothing? Feeling paranoid, I showed my handler out and fixed myself another drink now that I was alone, wondering if it had been drugged. Maybe I was becoming paranoid. Certainly, if I crossed Grump, I had much to fear, but so far, everyone seemed to think highly of me, wanting my favor. Perhaps I had nothing to fear.

Yet. It didn't take much to get killed here.

Alone at last, I gazed out the window toward Mt. Grumpmore. It stood nearly four thousand feet tall on an island just northeast of the capital and could be seen from everywhere, the likely reason the emperor had chosen it to grace us all with his presence. Not four, but five different busts of his head and chest had been carved into it. Each was hundreds of feet tall. From left to right they showed him peaceful, smiling, and dignified beneath his crown; haughtily looking down his nose in disapproval; smug and grinning; leering lewdly; and finally, angry and shouting with his mouth agape, one finger pointing at you. I had seen the mountain since arriving but not had the chance to admire it fully. No matter where one stood, the eyes of all five appeared to be following you.

I hadn't been there long when the TV sprang to life, a smug Shawn Handitty referring to the audience as "comrade," as Grump, Svetlana, and others had done. He prattled on about my arrival, various footage of my activities being shown that day. I hadn't seen cameras and now knew hidden ones were everywhere, likely always recording. Knowing someone could be watching even now, I feigned a smile at the broadcast, and when Grump repeated "Treasonous United Colonies," I loudly said, "Hail Grump!" in my suite, just in case. After Hannity's fawning program, during which he repeatedly referred to Grump as a stable genius and other flattering terms, a propaganda film came on, a voice-over reminding me that all citizens were required to watch it. I suspected everyone had seen it before.

What followed was a series of reminders about how great Grump was; what he'd done for everyone; how rich he was and that everything he'd achieved had been without any help from anyone, ever; how he'd beaten Crooked Hillary in 2016; how he was the greatest president, golfer, negotiator, etc.; how the U.C. Democrats had tried to steal the election results, attempted a coup, performed the greatest witch hunt in Amnesian history, and other plots against him, all of which he'd easily overcome; how much he was like his people and that they would one day earn a place in the Inner Party alongside his family, etc.; and his skill in golf – he apparently made 19 holes-in-one every time he played golf on his primary course here, with the extra hole.

Finally, the broadcast ended with a warning that evil forces in the Treasonous United Colonies (which was to say every last person there) were planning an attack on Grumpland and that, in the unlikely event this attack could not be repelled (because Grump was the greatest military mind in the history of the world and superior weaponry abounded), that everyone was to drink their vial of wine and join His Majesty in the afterlife, where everything they dreamed of would exist, courtesy of Donald J. Grump. A video of his pyramid, which I had yet to see up close, showed him ascending to heaven to be a god. Then the screen went dark, leaving this final message lingering in the mind.

Despite my relief that the broadcast was over, I tried to look disappointed that I couldn't hear anymore. I'd had a long day, but my mind was so awake that I despaired of ever getting off to sleep, so I decided to take a stroll on my own. The emperor had told me to make myself at home, so I felt almost obligated to be seen doing just that, though I hoped to avoid people and their conversations. With a glass of brandy in one hand, I exited my suite to find the hallway empty. For twenty minutes, I meandered through gilded halls, seeing few people and speaking with ever fewer.

My mind wandered over the day's events. My thoughts were interrupted as I passed yet another golden door and it opened to reveal a sexy brunette, who stood gazing at me through yellow-tinted protective glasses that made her look like a librarian, her ruby lips parted so that her tongue slowly licked over them. She wore a skin-tight, crotchless, black leather teddy and held a whip in one hand. High-heeled leather boots reached her knees. Her breasts strained at the fabric, two half-moon globes rising and falling with her sultry breath. She was otherwise bare. A moment passed before I recognized her.

"Sara Paylon?" I asked.

She took a step forward and, with one hand, grabbed my crotch. "You know what GOP stands for?" she purred. I hesitated, certain she'd say something other than what I'd heard. "Grab Our Penises," she finished. Then she yanked me into her rooms and slammed the doors behind us.

Having let go of me, the former Governor of Alaska sauntered toward the bed, looked back at me, and bent over to unzip the boots as I tried to avert my gaze but found myself unable. Only when she stepped out of them and moved for a decanter of wine did I tear my eyes away. Her rooms were full of divans, lace fabrics, and exotic animal trophies. On the bed's far side, a fireplace roared and crackled. She returned to me and handed me one of two pewter goblets filled with scented, mulled wine, bidding me to drink. Having finished my brandy, I complied, mesmerized and a little drunk already. She pulled me toward the four-post bed.

"Aren't those goggles for hunting?" I asked, trying to find something to say. Certainly, she didn't need them here.

"Yes, and now I have found my prey." She pushed me onto the bed and began to disrobe me with her teeth.

"So, uh, how was your day?" I asked lamely, wondering what to do.

"Not nearly as satisfying as my night will be."

Seeing weapons that looked freshly used, and camouflage clothing carelessly strewn about the floor, I asked, "Were you on Grump's Safari? I hear it's exciting."

With a skillful yank that suggested she had done this before, such was her expertise, she ripped my pants and underwear off in a single motion. "I had two kills."

I backed away on the bed, but she climbed on top of me. "What do you do with your prey once finished?"

She gestured with her head toward the fireplace. I looked over and there, on a bearskin rug, where I hadn't seen them before because the bed blocked my view, were the remains of two men, one black and one Latino, one riddled with bullets, the other appearing to have a single, clean shot through his forehead. "Don't worry, sweetie. I wouldn't do that to you. They were Democrats."

"Right."

She began rubbing her body along mine and the heat far surpassed what roared in the fireplace. There had been reports of the ice sheet on Grumpland melting and I jokingly mused that I now knew why. Sara Paylon, "She of the Fiery Loins," was too close to it. Had I been drugged again? My thoughts were broken by her next words, said to me in a low, guttural voice like a demon possessed her. Perhaps a succubus.

Chapter 6 – "Summer Camp"

"Take me now, sub creature."

Sarah's lips crushed mine and I surrendered.

She ravished me long into the night, insatiable as she was, before finally curling up beside me. I had lost all sense of time and place and fell into a deep slumber until the sunlight streamed in at the dawn. To my surprise, she had gone from the bed without a word (or another romp), but as I pulled my clothes back onto my sore body, I heard the playful splash of water from the bathroom and her soft singing of the Grump National Anthem, the words changed alluringly. I crept out of her rooms.

On my way back to my suite, those members of the Inner Party that I passed praised my disheveled hair and the pink lipstick that I wore all over my face and beyond. With a wink and a grin that made me turn crimson, they congratulated me and wished me a day to match my night. I found myself relieved on reaching my rooms, where I showered. The routine of this and dressing almost made me forget the horrors of the day before. It all seemed almost a dream or nightmare and I tried to shut it from my mind as I ate a quiet, solitary breakfast with my back to Mt. Grumpmore. But nothing lasts forever, and Svetlana arrived to collect me.

"I know what you did last night." She strode in and appraised me. "I wasn't sure you'd be functioning this morning, but it's good that you are. We're off to visit the districts."

"Where do the slaves live?" I asked, curious but afraid of what I'd learn about their living conditions.

"Yes. We have four of them, as we segregate slaves. We tend to nickname districts. District One is for the blacks. Right now, Ghettoville is popular for that one. Then there's District Two, or Wetbackia, for the Mexicans."

"And the gays?"

"Fagland, of course. That's District Three. And then there's my favorite name for District Four. Islame."

After a moment, I guessed, "For Muslims?"

"That's right!"

I smiled my feigned approval and we soon cruised down the highway in a golden limo that indicated our superior status. Some of our trip was to take place via helicopter and include a tour of the island. I'd get my first real look at someone other than the Inner Party and those Outer Party members stationed at the palace. I felt like I'd already seen a skewed version of life here and wondered if it was to be as awful as the day before had suggested. Since I'd been recommending this place to people for a decade without knowing what I was getting them into, I felt some responsibility for their living conditions and was both eager and dreading to learn more.

Svetlana explained that the districts weren't where all the slaves were because many were throughout the island on various assignments, where they had temporary quarters, but the only true home for them was in the districts. These were next to each other in four quadrants of a circle, miles in circumference, and a thick wall with armed guards surrounding it. She boasted that no one ever escaped, but slaves sometimes went missing and they couldn't figure out how this was happening; it was a well-guarded secret, one that piqued my interest.

We turned off the main road, heading further inland into a bleak valley with natural stone jutting high above the earth, forming a cliff on every side but the one from which we approached. It would be a rough climb for anyone wanting to escape the districts that way. Two armored trucks joined us, one before and one behind, filled with soldiers, and as the giant district walls loomed overhead, the thick gate slowly opened to admit us.

There wasn't much to see, and we didn't get out as we toured each identical district on dirt roads, where mud puddles and potholes abounded. Grump had built the place since arriving a decade ago, so the walls of buildings were still in good condition, but the first sign that there was no electricity were the clotheslines. Buildings were unadorned except for the Grump "T" everywhere. I was almost surprised to see glass windows but then the winters were tough this far north and Grump likely didn't care for his slaves dying off en masse. Every chimney seemed to belch smoke into the air. We only stopped in the black district because I recognized an unusually well-dressed slave standing on a wall and addressing a small crowd before him.

"Is that Kahnye West?" I asked, remembering he'd been a strong Grump supporter and even visited the White House when Grump was president.

Svetlana nodded. "CBG was the very first slave here, and he is their leader across all the districts. After all, as he noted long ago, slavery is a choice, and he's decided that the best way to serve the emperor is to make sure all the slaves obey and work hard."

I shook my head in amazement. "He voluntarily became a slave? Remarkable. Why do you call him CBG?"

"Oh, it stands for Christian Billionaire Genius, a name he once considered giving himself, though he was neither a genius nor a billionaire. His Majesty liked the name, so that's what he's called now."

"But isn't he penniless?"

"Yes, comrade, that's part of the joke. He's also a Muslim now, so we sometimes make him live in that district. He's King of the Slaves. Not really, of course. We just make fun of him and sometimes call him 'my lord.' He doesn't seem to realize he's being mocked."

Somehow that didn't surprise me. He had almost as much hubris as Grump. I couldn't hear the sermon he appeared to be giving, but I saw another familiar figure there. Svetlana did, too.

"Your Ebony Girl," she began, teasing me, "from the welcome ceremony, is over there."

"Yes, I see her."

"Why don't you go talk to her? You can make her do anything you want. Anything."

Pretending to be amused, I frowned and replied, "I prefer my woman to *want* to do something."

She rolled her eyes, still smiling. "You don't have to do that here. Take what you want, when you want."

"It's a little surprising to hear a woman talk this way."

She shrugged. "I know my place. Let's go talk to her."

Before I could stop her, she opened the car door and started in Ebony Girl's direction. I reluctantly followed, hoping she didn't make such remarks about using her for sex in front of the woman. By way of introducing me, she only informed Ebony Girl that she was to obey me in all things. I almost smiled apologetically but wiped the look from my face. Wishing Svetlana wasn't there to embarrass me further, I made a suggestion.

"Maybe she and I can talk inside for a few minutes."

My handler rolled her eyes again. "Yes, by all means, go inside and 'talk' with her."

I pretended to look amused as I followed the slave into the nearest building and closed the door behind us. She still hadn't spoken and remained silent as I observed Svetlana through a window while she went to sit on the hood of the limo. Then I turned back to Ebony Girl, who stood patiently in the kitchen with me, as if awaiting instruction.

"Do you live in a place like this?" I asked, gesturing around us.

"Yes, master," she replied in a pleasing accent that reminded me of West Africa. "We all do."

"Please don't call me that. I'm not comfortable with that. Um, how many to a house?"

"As many as will fit, mast-" She stopped herself.

Her reply didn't surprise me. "How many is that usually?"

"Two dozen, maybe three."

Back in the U.C., less than six would've lived here, in normal circumstances. I got up and went to a cupboard, opening it to find worn wooden plates and bowls. Cutlery was no better and I saw no appliances of any kind due to the lack of electricity. Candles stood out of the way, since it was daytime, but all looked well used. The floors were dirt. There was no plumbing or a sink, and when I asked, she confirmed there was no running water and they had to get it from a well. Food was cooked outside using firepits everyone shared. I asked her for a tour of the house, worried what I'd see, and found that for a toilet, they had only a bedpan they had to empty outside. Bedrooms had no mattresses or beds so that they slept on the dirt floor under blankets that were well worn, torn, but at least of appropriate thickness. Grump had them living, if you could call it that, in abject poverty.

"Every home is the same, you say?"

"Yes."

"In the other districts, too?"

"Yes."

"Where do you bathe?"

"A bathhouse nearby mast... my lord There is one for each district. We're allowed to use it once a week."

I looked her over, noting her superior cleanliness compared to the other slaves I'd already seen, except Kahnye. "You don't have to call me 'my lord' either. Does everyone bathe that infrequently?"

"No. Some of us can more often."

"And you are one of them?"

"Yes."

"Why?"

"His Majesty fancies me. It's a great honor."

I let myself frown. "Does he come here often?"

"No. Never. If he wants a given slave, we are brought to him."

That didn't surprise me, but I didn't much care about that and had been working my way up to my real question, trying to put her at ease first so she didn't become defensive. "I saw you at the ceremony yesterday. You kept looking at me. Why?"

She bowed her head again. "I beg your pardon."

"It's okay. It didn't bother me. I was just curious about you."

After a pause, she admitted, "And I was curious about you."

"Why?"

"They say you are the man who sends everyone here."

I pursed my lips. My role in the formation of Grumpland was an increasingly ignoble one, and I suddenly wondered how many proles hated my guts or if they truly believed everything would be wonderful, like I'd told them, and Grump continued to claim despite the truth. "And you're curious what I'm like?" I guessed.

"Yes."

"And you want to know why I would send people here?" I had to admit, I was starting to feel defensive, but it wasn't because of anything she'd said, just my conscience.

She looked uncomfortable, as if unsure how to respond, so I waved that off, but then she spoke up. "You are not what I expected. That is why I kept looking at you."

"In what way?"

She hesitated and then admitted, "You have kind eyes."

This struck me as a daring comment, for if it was assumed that I'd known what was going on here, I was presumably on board with the evil I now witnessed. I asked an obvious question. "That surprises you?"

"No one here has kind eyes." She looked away as if remembering someone else.

"Except...?"

She flashed a small, sheepish smile that I'd read her. "The other slaves, when we are alone."

"What are your relationships like?"

She shrugged as if not sure how to explain, so I let her think. "We are family. We take of each other. No one else can."

"What happens when one of you is sick or injured?"

She again seemed reluctant to answer until I reassured her that I was only seeking the truth and wasn't judging that truth. I could find out from others but wanted to hear it from her. I didn't mean to imply that if she lied, I'd find out, but I sensed that I'd done so from the way she lifted her head, looked me in the eye, and now answered plainly.

"It depends on how serious it is. Those who cannot work do not have value. Some are given light duties while they recover. Most are killed."

I suspected as much but failed to hide my disapproval. "Even if they could recover?"

"Sometimes, yes."

"How? How are they killed?"

"It depends on the mood of the guards. Some are stripped and stabbed, the clothes given to another. Others are starved in a pit, but other slaves sometimes tossed food down to them at night, so we are kept away now. Slaves were punished for helping someone this way."

"Punished how?" I felt certain I knew the answer.

"Death."

I put my head in my hands. I might not have been responsible for slaves being brought here, but I certainly bore the guilt for those who'd enslaved them and treated them this way. I was not alone in looking the other way at Grump's bigotry, but I now stood out as the chief perpetrator. I had never believed it would cause such a thing. I felt ashamed and stupid for the crap I'd been repeating.

I don't know how long I stood there, lost in thought, but when I looked up, I found Ebony Girl watching me, a smile in her eyes. "You are not like the others," she said approvingly.

I sighed and nodded without pleasure.

"Better go back to pretending that you are until you leave this place." To my startled look, it was her turn to smile knowingly, having read me.

"You won't tell?" I asked rhetorically, knowing she wouldn't.

"No."

I was going to ask her more when Svetlana called from outside that we needed to get going. I yelled that I'd be right out and turned back to Ebony Girl.

"Keep yourself safe here. If anyone asks what we talked about, it was only your life here, and that of the others, and that you told me the truth about whatever I asked. Don't risk yourself for me. I'll tell them I was very pleased with our talk."

She seemed to accept that, and I walked back out into the cold air, finding Svetlana smirking. I endured some jokes about how I didn't look "spent" and I fended off questions about whether I'd at least kissed Ebony Girl. I only considered it now that she'd said it, a fact that Svetlana noticed and teased me about before changing the subject as we left the districts behind.

"We're going to do an island tour," she began, "but first we're stopping in town so you can see Princess Ivanaka. She's to do a reading today for some preschoolers. We've proud of our education system. It's the best in the world. Everyone says so."

"I'm looking forward to seeing it." This was actually true, as I wondered what they were being taught, though I suspected the sinister teachings were being saved for grade school and beyond. But then perhaps they'd surprise me.

The town itself was certainly better than the districts, since items existed that we'd consider basic in many places, such as electricity. I saw no cars, however, with Svetlana explaining that people lived close to their jobs and didn't need to go far, and if they did, a community-owned bike suited them fine. They didn't own much or need to buy anything like supplies and food, for Grump provided everything. As a result, there were no stores either, just row upon row of townhouses, all identical and colorless. I only saw a few people outside, all wearing the same outfit. Each was engaged in tidying up the exterior of a building or lawn.

We soon turned off the main highway onto yet another road that had Grump's name on it, where a large building before us grew nearer. She informed me that it was for all grades up through 6th, and that formal schooling ended there. Nothing more was considered needed for anyone, whether proles, the Outer Party, or the Inner Party. There were no colleges in Grumpland.

This arrangement kept people from showing too much imagination or initiative, according to Svetlana. I knew it also prevented them from ever leaving the island and having a viable option elsewhere. That inspired me to ask what happened if someone wanted to leave, but she shot me such a withering look that I knew the answer to be that anyone dumb enough to suggest left alright... in a body bag. When I asked about holidays, she admitted that no one leaves for that either because Grumpland provides for every need. Besides, the rest of the world was evil and hated them for their superiority.

We exited the car and walked past a typically manicured lawn with statues of Grump. The menacing, hulking building before us doubled as a dormitory so that the kids could be educated all day, immersed in Grump's teachings. This was considered comprehensive and a true sign of Grump's love for his people, so the parents were thrilled and had little to do but come visit from time to time, though she claimed most didn't because they knew Grump loved their kids even more than they did and they wanted everyone to think of him as their father. Empress Telania was also known affectionately as the Queen Mother (because Empress Mother didn't roll off the tongue quite as well).

Regardless, according to my handler, this parental separation didn't scar the children at all and instead built strength and independence. Many parents simply let their kids be taken away at an early age and then moved on with their lives, confident that everything would be fine in Grump's capable hands. This explained the general absence of children under a certain age everywhere else I'd gone. They were all confined to Grump Wealth Institute of Technology (TWIT), as it was called, despite being an elementary school. All students, past or present (even future) were called a TWIT; these were also divided into star rankings, depending on grade reached. A six-star TWIT was in 6th grade. Graduates were TWITters, despite that being the name of a much-hated social media platform everywhere but in Grumpland, where their own service, Grumper, existed instead; everyone was required to use it and "like" each of the emperor's "trumps" immediately.

As fascinating as I found these details, I especially looked forward to getting inside, looking around, and watching

Princess Ivanaka interact with these children. We soon found her with an entourage of a dozen helpers, including both slaves and Outer Party members who ran the school. They stood gathered around a cake with white icing and an image of her father's face dominating almost the entire thing.

"It's lovely," said Ivanaka, looking radiant in a yellow dress, high heels, and a fortune in jewelry adorning nearly everything: fingers, wrists, neck, earlobes, ankles, in her hair, and more. "Wonderful job, ladies. The kids will be so happy to see it."

A chorus of thanks erupted from the lips of those in attendance. Then they wheeled the cake into a nearby room as the rest of us followed.

To my handler, I quietly remarked, "That was very nice of her to bring them this cake."

Svetlana whispered to me, "It's against the law to damage any image of His Majesty."

I looked at her in surprise. "Then how are they supposed to eat it?"

"There was a small portion of it there in the corner. Did you see?"

I nodded, having seen an area approximately two squares inches in size. How this was to feed a group of children I couldn't fathom. Perhaps this one was for show and another cake didn't have Grump's visage ruining it, but there wasn't one.

I followed the princess and Svetlana into the room, where the children already sat on a threadbare carpet with that genitalia-like capital T embroidered on it. An elegant rocking chair had been placed before them for Ivanaka, who sat there while smiling coolly at her audience. Her nose had wrinkled into a perceptible sneer as if she regarded something disgusting, her brown eyes not lingering on them. Around the room stood a dozen guards, making me wonder what she had to fear from the two dozen toddlers. Awaiting all of us with a big smile was Kierstyn Nealson, the former U.C. Secretary of Homeland Security.

But what most caught my eye was the malnourished appearance of all the boys and girls. Their arms and legs were thin. Cheeks were sunken. Eyes were hollow and vacant with despair, though these lit up on seeing Princess Ivanaka. Each wore a vial of that red liquid around their necks; some of them were absentmindedly playing with theirs. Unwashed hair brought attention to their often ill-fitting clothing that had seen better days, much of it had holes, tears, or was just mismatched, like a boy with different colored socks, one long and one short. I could smell them from where I stopped beside my handler.

"Children," began Kierstyn, "Her Majesty has brought all of you a delicious cake to eat. What do you say?" They loudly and repeatedly said their thanks, wishing much good fortune on Ivanaka in return. "She's going to read to you about her father, our wonderful emperor, and then we'll have the treat."

With that, Ivanaka opened a golden book on her lap.

"This story is called *The Golden Emperor*," she began. "Once upon a time, a very stable genius was born into this world. He was a gifted athlete and smarter than anyone who'd ever lived. Even as a baby, women loved him, and boys wanted to be like him. His name was Donald J. Grump.

"As special as he was, life wasn't always easy for him. He started off poor, without a ruble to his name, and was abandoned by both his mother and father, who were both jealous of how wonderful he was. Forced to live on the street, he counted animals among his best friends. They would bring him nuts and berries for him to live on. And while he survived, it was a sad and lonely life.

"But fortune soon smiled upon him. He rescued a kitten from a tree one day, then found a lost puppy on the road. The owners of these pets were so grateful that they paid him handsomely. It seemed that he had found his calling, and for years thereafter, he roamed the streets, often taking dangerous jobs to rescue animals and people from terrible fates that had befallen them. He came to be adored by all, but even this brought problems.

"People were so jealous of him that they sought to destroy him at every turn. Older, meaner children tried to beat him up, but what they didn't know is that he swings back twice as hard as them, and so he left a trail of broken and ruined bodies in his wake. The girlfriends of those bullies were so aroused by his strength, cunning, and courage that they threw themselves at him, showering kisses upon him. He made love to as many as he pleased and began fathering his own brood of wonderful children that would need homes.

"And this was how he entered into the real estate business. With no money at all, he used his bare hands to build homes instead of relying upon skilled laborers, who'd fall short of his magnificence anyway. Grump Tower was the tallest and most glorious building the world had ever seen. He and his children moved in, and rich people from all over wanted to as well, so he let them, becoming the wealthiest person anyone had ever known.

"But he didn't stop there. Other people from all walks of life would benefit from his great gift, his stable genius, and so instead of spending his days in idle luxury (or playing golf), he personally built more and more towers, palaces, and gilded halls throughout the world."

As Ivanaka turned another gold-leafed page, one of the little girls began to cry for unknown reasons. The princess paused a moment, shooting a cold look at the girl before trying to continue, but the girl kept crying. It grew louder. Finally, with an expressionless glance at Kierstyn, Ivanaka calmly folded the book closed in her lap, sighed ever so slightly, and raised her gaze to an invisible point above the children's heads. Kierstyn stepped forward to the little girl, shushing her gently and smiling, but the girl cried on. Kierstyn made her lie down on her back. Then she put one hand over the girl's mouth and pinched her nose closed with the other.

"Shhh," she repeated. "It's alright. You're going to summer camp in the sky now and just need to sleep first. Would you like that?"

The girl didn't react to this, other than to pull her little hands up to Kierstyn's and try to pry them from her nose and mouth so she could breathe. Kierstyn let go long enough to straddle the girl, whose arms she pinned with her knees. Then she resumed the suffocation. The girl squirmed, but it was her vocal protests that caused a sigh of annoyance from Her Highness. In response, Kierstyn began softly singing "Baby Shark." The tune was familiar to the other kids, and after a verse, one of them quietly chimed in. Then another, and another, and soon all the kids were singing it as the little girl's face turned blue, her eyes bulged, and little sounds of protest failed to break through the music all around her. I guessed this was the purpose of the singing.

At last, Kierstyn let go of her baby shark death grip and checked the little girl's pulse. It was clear to anyone watching that she was quite dead. Kierstyn agreed and rose, straightening her outfit, before looking at the remaining children.

"Does anyone else want to go to summer camp?" Kierstyn asked them. With wide eyes, white faces, and barely controlled alarm, they silently shook their heads. Seemingly satisfied, Kierstyn returned to her place as a guard unceremoniously dragged the corpse away by one tiny ankle, a trail of rock-hard breadcrumbs falling out of one pocket. Another kid eyed them but apparently thought better of helping herself to them.

Only now did I realize that Ivanaka was silently fuming, her ruby lips set in a tight line, eyes hard, posture rigid. She stiffly rose to her feet, cold eyes sweeping across the children.

"My father," she began haughtily, "did not suffer so greatly only to be looked at with pity, but to be admired as a god. I am bitterly disappointed that you cannot wait until the story's end to see his shining example of overcoming adversity to be the greatest man who has ever lived. And so, it is that you will suffer this day, as he once did. There will be no cake for any of you. You are not deserving! And to think this morning I thought, in the kindness of my great heart, 'Let them eat cake.' But now my heart knows only coldness for you. Weep. Weep now for my benevolence in teaching you this valuable lesson."

On cue, the children burst into genuine tears and I stifled a sigh of relief. For a minute there, I'd thought she intended to have them all killed. Instead, she reserved that for their teachers, who were rounded up by the guards and brought onto the lawn visible outside the room. They were stripped naked so as not to ruin clothes that would be given to others. Thin and malnourished like their pupils, they begged for forgiveness, praising the princess and the emperor, but there was no mercy here. The guards began knifing them (to save bullets, Svetlana whispered to me) in full view of the children, continuing to stab long after each body had fallen and lay motionless in a pool of blood.

A powerful lesson had been taught and I knew those kids would never forget it. I had led their parents here. I felt sick. There was nothing decent that Grump and his loyal family couldn't turn into something hideous, even a cake for preschoolers. The princess calmly walked out with her cold serenity restored. The children continued to wail as the guards and Kierstyn left them behind. Only I and Svetlana remained. I kept my face turned away from her because I knew a blank mask or look of approval wasn't coming. Only when other staff at the school came in to soothe the children did I begin to calm down.

As Svetlana and I left for other parts of the school, I saw a staff member wheel the cake from the toddler room and toss the rest of it into the trash. I blanked my expression lest they see the hate in my eyes. To be cruel to adults was one thing, but they surpassed what was tolerable. I could hardly stand the idea of seeing more shown to me, and yet there was no escape.

We soon reached a room where Shawn Handitty, a former Fox opinion host, stood teaching a group of first graders about how Democrats in the U.C. were evil, hated them, and were out to destroy all of them. He clearly believed it by the fervor in his eyes, where I thought I saw madness. Story after story rolled from his mouth. Some were familiar to me, but others piled on the pending apocalypse that Grump had been threatening since before moving here. We continued to another class, this time third grade, and found Pucker Karlson doing much the same thing, reminding the kids of their pledge to drink the poisoned wine at the right time and join His Majesty in the next world. It seemed that everywhere we looked, predictions of doom and Emperor Grump being the only salvation were at hand.

This helped explain two other scenes we encountered. In one, a lovely, smiling girl of about eight years sat beside a dollhouse, playing with a figure of Grump and another of a voluptuous blonde woman in skimpy clothes. She was alone. When I asked why, Svetlana told the girl to tell me herself, so she did.

"I'm the best princess in my class today," said the girl.

"That's great," I responded, happy to see something pleasant going on at least somewhere. "What did you do to become the best?"

"My essay about was how much I love His Majesty."

I stifled an eye-roll. "What did it say?"

"How I hope to be his favorite girl in the GOP Rooms one day."

At times like this, I was glad that Svetlana wasn't looking directly at me until my startled reaction had passed, at least outwardly. Surely this girl didn't know what happened in a GOP Room. I struggled for a way to ask and then decided I didn't want to know. I'd only feel worse if she somehow knew.

In a room a few doors down, a sobbing boy stood before a blackboard, writing, "Bad boys are sent to Amnesia" over and over. I failed to hide my concern over his anguish, prompting Svetlana to tease me.

"It's okay," she whispered to me. "We don't actually send anyone back."

"Then why is he writing it?"

"Fear."

I supposed that summed everything in Grumpland. "What do you do instead?"

She smirked. "Send them to summer camp."

I arched an eyebrow, thinking she was kidding, and then feared what might happen if someone saw the terrified boy crying this way. As he started writing the sentence over again, he saw us from the corner of his eyes and turned white. I didn't have to be told he'd seen people killed for nothing. Unable to help myself, I walked toward him, trying to placate him with my open hands and gentle voice as I told him everything was okay. He looked fearfully over my shoulder at Svetlana, who I asked to leave us alone for a minute, pretending that, as a reporter supporting them, I wanted to learn more from the boy. This was partly true, as I did want to know what had happened, but in this evil place, the boy's tears were the only honesty around and I felt drawn to his despair, which tugged at my compassion when so many around me were so cold. I sensed in him a kindred spirit in that he was someone for whom pain still mattered.

"It's okay," I began, down on one knee beside him. I positioned myself so Svetlana couldn't sneak in behind me without me seeing her do so. "You can stop writing for a minute."

"Okay," he said, voice weak and trembling. The immediate obedience caught my attention.

"Who has you writing this?"

"Professor Karlson."

"Why?"

"I'm a bad boy."

I bit my lip, wanting to tell him otherwise but worried about how that might cause him trouble of some kind if he subsequently showed defiance to someone who told him that. I wondered how much abuse was being heaped upon all of them, and for what. "What did you do?"

"It's not what I did. It's what I am."

I inadvertently glared at this sentiment having been taught to him and the boy thought my anger was directed at him, for he started crying more and apologizing, causing me to put one comforting hand on his back as I shushed him.

"I'm not angry with you, son. I'm upset that someone has taught you this. It's okay. You're not a bad boy. I don't want you to believe this about yourself. You're a child and have things to learn. Mistakes are bound to happen, even innocent ones."

The boy started crying more, a flood of tears drenching his cheeks, and I sensed I was perhaps the first person ever showing him compassion and understanding. I pulled him closer and put an arm around him, telling him more of the same things and wondering how far to go with it. If he had learned to clamp down on his heart to protect himself, then me opening it up for him might backfire in the long run. Was there any way to stop these things from happening? I'd never get him or anyone else off this island, and even if I somehow could, could they ever be saved? How far had they been brainwashed? Even as I thought it, I knew myself to be a perpetrator and hung my head.

Svetlana cleared her throat from the hall, and I knew I had to go. The boy clung to me so that I had to gently pry his arms from my neck. I wiped the tears from his face and told him to keep writing as he'd been instructed to do, but to not believe what he wrote, or bad things about himself if someone repeated them. He asked if he could come with me, but I said I could not but would try to visit him again if I could.

"What is your name?" I asked him.

"Donald."

I stifled a frown, remembering Grump's edict about people taking his name. "Is that what you were always called?"

He hesitated, then whispered, "No."

"What's your birth name?"

He paused again and I had to coax it out of him. "David."

"Well David, I'll see what I can do for you, okay?"

He nodded but it seemed like the light of hope had gone out of his eyes. I gave him a final pat on the back. As I rose and started for the door, I almost felt faint at the fate of these children. Suddenly I felt sick and raced to the nearest trash can, vomiting into it so that Svetlana came in to see what was the matter with me. I claimed it was my breakfast, only to hear her remark that she'd find out who'd prepared it and have them beaten. I puked again, then told her not to do that, and to keep it between me and her. Behind me, I heard David continuing to write on the chalkboard and as I struggled to my feet, I gave him one final look before leaving with my handler. Realizing that half the kids here had the same name, I told her now that I wanted to see him again to learn more about his life here, and she agreed to arrange it, taking his photo with her iGrump.

Since I was feeling ill, she didn't fight my suggestion that we see no more of the school. Svetlana and I returned to the car in silence as I reflected on what I'd seen. The abominations of Grumpland were only growing and we had a helicopter tour of the island next. The idea relieved me, for I could presumably only see so much horror from above.

"It's time for you to see the Eight Wonders of Grumpland," she said.

Chapter 7 – "Ebony Girl"

"Eight wonders?" I asked Svetlana as we approached a waiting helicopter.

"Yes, comrade, one more than the Seven Wonders of the Ancient World. They are throughout the island."

"What are they?"

"Well, you've already seen the palace with its estate grounds. That includes another wonder you've already enjoyed, in the GOP Room. Then there's the statue at the harbor. I'll show you the pyramid soon, and we may have time for you to gamble at Grump's Emperor Casino. You saw Mount Grump-more from your rooms? Good. We should visit Grumpland Amusement Park on our tour today. And of course, there's The Wall."

And as it turns out, that was one of our first destinations. We flew past Port Grump, where the Golden Cruise ship was just leaving for Amnesia, passing beneath the giant Grump statue. As I'd noticed before, a wall surrounded the land here along the coast, but rather than being a thousand meters tall, it was fifty feet at its highest point. Moreover, as we flew along the coast and out of sight from the settlements, the wall disappeared altogether.

"Maybe I misheard," I began to Svetlana, "but I thought the Emperor had said the whole island is surrounded by a wall a thousand meters tall."

"That's the plan. We're still building it. We've only completed the sections near the inhabited areas. It's a very ambitious project. It's going to be beautiful. The best ever."

"But aren't the immigrants most likely to come ashore in uninhabited places and then make their way to the cities and towns?"

She frowned and ducked my question. "We need the proles to see the progress we've made and feel safe from outside threats."

I saw no sign that any work was being done at all, which remained true as the miles fell behind us. There weren't even roads to reach the coast. We soared over a few other towns along the western coastline, and at each of them there stood the low wall. I doubted Grump really intended to build what he'd bragged about. It would be insanely expensive and, as he predicted, probably longer than the Great Wall of China. It also wasn't necessary. Any immigrant would be detectable at once due to an inability to fit in with the malnourished proles I'd seen and their blind subservience to Grump, a mental trait that I doubted anyone could easily fake at all or for long. The wall's existence was yet another lie.

My handler peppered me with minor details about everywhere we went. The land was bleak and hostile, like its new people, but moments of beauty were to be found. She took me on tours of gorgeous peaks and ice flows, finally arriving at the ice sheet covering much of Grumpland. West and south of us were the green and brown fields of the island, but to the north and west lay an expanse of snow and ice that seemed to go on forever. I remarked as such to Svetlana, wondering what we could possibly be going to see.

"That," she replied, pointing down.

Growing larger by the moment was what appeared to be a complex of low buildings that stood on the edge between land

and ice. A blaze of fire seemed to roar beneath each, and yet a torrent of water rushed beneath them and toward a nearby lake. To one side of that water body flowed a wide river that gushed over the landscape on its way to the Arctic Sea. As we neared, I saw that the buildings were no such thing. Rather, they were enormous machines on treads. Each was moving ever so slowly onto the ice sheet, which was disappearing beneath them as they melted it away.

"What is this?" I asked, alarmed at the melting. Perhaps Sara Paylon wasn't responsible after all.

"The Grumpland Reclamation Project. His Majesty is reclaiming the rest of this land for exploitation."

"Exploiting for what?"

"Whatever he thinks of next! The empire also needs more land due to the growing population. We expect to be the most populous country soon."

That seemed dubious on a number of levels, but we'd already passed over so much uninhabited land that there was simply no need to reclaim more. "Isn't all this melted ice going to raise the sea level?"

"Yes! That's part of his very stable genius. He can not only reclaim this lost land, but by the time we've melted the entire ice sheet, the global sea level will have risen twenty-three feet!"

I knew that even a foot would be a world-wide disaster. "Why is that desirable?"

"Two reasons. First, the ice sheet helps keep the Earth at its current temperature. By melting it, we will raise global temperatures so that much life on Earth will be wiped out everywhere but here. This is one way we can destroy our enemies."

"That's very clever," I admitted, feeling dread overcome me. They were mad, and surely life on Grumpland would also perish. "What's the other reason?"

"When sea levels rise that much, we'll destroy the coastline of every major country, and most of the shit holes ones, too. Most important cities are on the coast so we can devastate all other powers, leaving us as supreme!"

"Won't that kill a lot of people?"

"Hopefully! The emperor has planned this well, along with our Minister of Architecture, Evo. All of our settlements and ports have been rebuilt on higher ground in anticipation."

"How long does he expect this to take?"

"At our current rate, about another thirty years."

"Won't he be dead by then?"

"Yes, comrade, but we'll still have won."

"But aren't all of you supposed to kill yourselves and join him?"

"I don't follow you."

"Never mind."

By now we had circled the machines several times, but it was time to head back toward the palace. Along the way, we approached rollercoaster tracks looping above the tree line.

"This is another of the Eight Wonders," Svetlana began as we flew above it. "Grumpland Amusement Park."

The park seemed like any other I'd seen except that it appeared quite overgrown in places, especially along the perimeter. Peeling paint could be seen everywhere, including the rides. There were no people and it looked like no one had been there in years. Each time we passed a rollercoaster and other thrill rides, I noticed body parts at the base of the supporting infrastructure. They were mostly arms, or hands, and occasionally a severed head. The stray foot, often with shoes still on, dotted the grass. At first, I assumed these were leftover Halloween decorations from the previous year, but a few had carrion birds pecking away at them.

"Excuse me," I began, "are those body parts I see?"

She patted my leg affectionately. "Don't be silly. We have the best inspectors in the world. Safety is a top concern."

Adopting a polite tone, I pointed at a rickety Ferris wheel that was clearly tilted to one side. "Is that ride out of service?"

"Of course not. It's too popular. The kids love it."

"Have you ever been on it?"

She recoiled before chuckling. "No, silly. These rides are for the proles. The Inner Party sacrifices the joys this place offers so that the citizens can enjoy it. The whole park is recently closed for renovations. It's going to be better than ever. Everyone says so."

I didn't see anyone working on it and knew the look of something abandoned when I saw it. By contrast, our next stop bustled with activity and could also be seen from a distance. A tall pyramid soared into the sky, its surface covered in white stone that seemed to sparkle in the sun. I'd seen the Great Pyramid in Egypt and this was taller and even had an extra side, which meant it technically wasn't a pyramid after all, but I decided not to comment on this any more than I did on Grump's false claim that he was an emperor. This "pyramid" with five sides, another of his Eight Wonders, likely should've had another name such as "pentagon," but of course that was a building back in the U.C. and that would never do.

Slaves were hard at work on both the exterior and interior. Men with whips slashed at them even when a great effort was being expended. Though modern machinery was available to make this easier, it was all seemingly being built by hand. Men who couldn't work anymore were unceremoniously killed and dumped into a large pit of corpses that we flew over on our way to the top, where a landing pad awaited. This wasn't at the apex, but several stories down and on the rear side where fewer would see it. She informed me that this was where the emperor's body would be brought via helicopter before descending to the sarcophagus below. Once interred, that night, his spirit would ascend to a passing comet and through heaven's gate on its way to a new, greater existence.

I wasn't sure what to say about all of this and had been looking around while she spoke. To one side was a golden escalator that led up to the apex. Seeing my gaze, she informed me that no one was allowed to climb it, for only Grump's spirit could do so. But what struck me most was stack upon stack of gold bars beside this stairway to heaven.

"Why all the gold?"

"He's ensuring that he gets in, of course. Heaven will be his next acquisition once he gives God an offer he can't refuse."

Playing along, I asked, "And what if God does indeed refuse?"

"Then I guess it will be a hostile takeover! All Grumpers will automatically get in. His Majesty has already arranged a deal with Satan."

The repeated, sober references to the devil were beginning to make me wonder if they were telling the truth or just believed it. "For what?"

"All liberals, non-whites, and non-heteros will go straight to Hell."

"What did he have to trade for this deal?"

She looked genuinely puzzled for a moment. "Well, we're not supposed to say it out loud, so you never heard me say this, but it's common knowledge among the ruling class that, throughout his life, he has acted as Lucifer's most prolific champion. Satan is quite thrilled with his protégé, in fact. He even worried that His Majesty planned a hostile takeover of Hell. This was part of Emperor Grump's plan, of course."

"How so?"

"By making Satan fear that takeover of Hell, His Majesty manipulated Satan into suggesting Emperor Grump take over heaven instead, with help from the devil. The alternative was Grump replacing Satan."

"Clever."

"Yes. I'm sure the emperor would do better than Satan has in hell and, in fact, more corruption has taken place since Grump first became President than in all the millennia before that. Satan has been kind of sleeping on the job and can't match the furor of His Majesty."

I nodded, speechless.

She led me to an elevator that descended to the area that Svetlana said was the most important because it's where Grump's body would remain. In the Emperor's Chamber, we found several Latino slaves toiling away on carving an enormous granite sarcophagus. I couldn't make out the scenes or words with them being in the way, but they could hardly have been different from those lining the walls. Every statement heaped great praise upon Grump and was attributed to one ruler of a sovereign power or another. Each scene showed Grump in his viral prime, hunting, ruling, having adoring people worship him, and him mating with beautiful blonde women. Directing the slaves' work was a tall, balding white man with a long, flowing mustache.

Seeing my inquisitively arched eyebrow, Svetlana whispered to me, "That's Evo. He's the Minister of Architecture I told you about. He's a certified genius. This pyramid is built with cores of pure selenium, gold plated bolts, and magnesium-tungsten alloys. It will open a portal to a higher plane where Grump will become a god and all of us will follow him there."

Just then, her phone buzzed with a message that she was needed somewhere else and our tour would have to end early. I can't say I was disappointed. I'd seen enough.

Via the helicopter, Svetlana dropped me off at the palace, telling me there was a surprise from His Majesty awaiting me in my rooms, plus another from herself, with his approval; she'd arranged them during our return visit, via text message. I feigned excitement while privately worrying that trouble lay before me. I moved through the now-familiar halls alone, sometimes chatting with royals I met along the way. I avoided the hall where Sara Paylon lurked in her lair. When I reached my suite, I pushed open the door, once again concerned that my rooms could not be locked.

I stepped inside and closed the door behind me. My eyes immediately spotted an array of fast food laid out on the dining table. As I neared, it became clear that it was all from Grump's restaurants. A note next to it indicated he wanted me to sample it all and tell him what I thought, and to include my assessment in whatever reporting I did back in the Treasonous United

Colonies on my show. "Hail Grump," I muttered on finishing the note. Now I knew his surprise. But where was Svetlana's?

I moved about the suite and, on entering the bedroom, found her gift.

Ebony Girl lay under the bedsheets, propped up with her black hair fanned out on the pillow. Her shoulders were bare, and I sensed she was nude except for the black collar that nearly blended in with her neck due to its color and tightness; I wondered how hard it was to remove. She smiled at me, revealing the stark white teeth, but I noticed that this expression didn't touch her eyes. A slave, she was required to do what I commanded, and I wondered what orders my handler had given her. While I found her alluring, I didn't want her this way. Not unless it was her own free will. I returned her smile and approached, stopping inches from the bed. She began to lower the sheet to bare her breasts, but I stopped her.

"Not yet," I began gently, struggling to find a way out of this predicament. "If you and I are to, uh, enjoy each other's company that way, it will be when it's your choice, and mine."

"It's not your choice now?" she asked.

"It might be. But it's not yours. Not yet."

"How do you know this? Perhaps it is all I dream of," she playfully suggested. I sensed some genuine humor behind the words and smiled.

"Call it a hunch." I glanced around and then asked, "Are you hungry? There's far more food out there than I can eat. I'd like you to join me."

"If you wish." She slipped her bare legs off to the side and I sensed she was about to stand nude before me. I stopped her with a raised palm.

"Please dress first, after I step outside. I'll give you a few moments. Take all the time you need. And if you don't want to join me, you don't have to. You have free will."

At this, she failed to stifle a brief frown. "I'm a slave. We do not have free will."

I sighed. "To me, you are not a slave. I know that may seem strange, but it's what I believe." In a hushed voice, I continued. "If I had the power to free you, I would, so for tonight, you are free as long as you are with me." I stopped there, wondering if this was enough. How long had she been a slave? Did she ever know freedom or were the words I said something she honestly couldn't fathom? Would she assume I was trying to trick her? The thought made my heart burn.

She gazed at me thoughtfully, clearly trying to read me and my intentions. "You are not from here."

I wasn't sure why she pointed it out, as we'd already covered that. "I am not. Just a visitor."

"But you would not have come unless you believed as His Majesty does."

So that was it. "I can see your reasoning..." I hesitated, choosing my words more carefully for fear the room was bugged. "But no two people agree on every last thing."

"Oh, the people here, Inner Party, Outer Party, the proles, they all agree with a uniformity that...that..."

"I understand and have seen it. But as you said, I'm not from here. Perhaps I still carry with me ideas from other places." I smiled.

She looked at me for several seconds before either accepting or pretending to accept this. "If it pleases you, I will play along. Maybe we'll come to believe in our little game."

I sighed again. "Whatever you like. Join me in a few minutes." I started for the door. Behind me, I heard her bare feet step on the floor and sensed that a backward glance would reveal everything. I stopped at the threshold and asked over one shoulder, "Do you have a name? Surely it's not Ebony Girl."

"You can call me whatever you like."

"Stop that," I said with some irritation.

She laughed, a beautiful, hearty alto. "My name is Jada, if it pleases you."

"It does."

"You may look. I am dressed."

I turned cautiously and found that she'd wrapped herself in a thin, silk, white robe that came to mid-thigh, her bountiful bosom stretching at the fabric, the twin bumps of her nipples daring my gaze, just like her cleavage and legs. The white fabric accentuated just how uniformly black her skin and hair were, like the night itself wore a robe and stood smiling at me.

Choosing my words, I said, "You look lovely in that, but I want you in more proper clothes...ones that don't make me hunger for something other than food," I teased. Only her shy look at the floor told me she was blushing, for with skin that dark, one couldn't possibly tell. "I can have someone send for something, if you'd like." She looked surprised and pleased, so I stepped out and used a phone to arrange it, struggling to guess at Jada's measurements and choose a style that seemed appropriate, but I had experience shopping for a woman before.

In less than five minutes, a servant arrived with a box of jewelry and five outfits, not just the one I'd requested, which was just as well; Jada could choose instead of me doing it for her. The servants knew how to please, at least. I sent her in to Jada and the girl left. A few minutes later, my companion stepped into the room in white high heels, a flowery dress hanging in folds to her ankles, around which were two golden bands. The demure, strapless dress bared her arms, one having a golden band wrapping around her bicep and ending with the dragon, two rubies for eyes. A matching pin swept back her long curls behind one ear, the hair on the other side tumbling over her bosom. A thin scarf hid the collar and dangled behind her.

As if afraid she'd be in trouble, she asked, "Is it too much? Should I take anything off?"

"No. Definitely not. Although you do seem overdressed for fast food."

She hesitated and I realized she didn't understand my attempt at humor. Waving off the remark, I motioned for her to come sit beside me at the table, curious about her life so I could gauge what to say and not. Only then did I realize I wanted to lighten the mood with some charm but couldn't tell whether a quip would fall flat or not. She was so lovely that I couldn't help being aware that I could already be intimate with her, but commanding someone to perform sex acts or tell you details of their life wasn't the same as having a conversation and feeling affection for someone. I wanted the connection, especially after all the awfulness I'd seen. If it led to sex, then so be it, but one was a goal, the other a fringe benefit. The measure of a man was which one he felt that way about.

It became apparent from her hesitation that leading the way was my role, so I chose an assortment of fries, nuggets, chicken wings, and other finger food for her and myself, serving us both. She still held back, but then the growl of her stomach made her blush and me laugh. With the ice broken, we began to eat and drink, Jada opening up more as we continued, and I began asking about herself. I learned that she hadn't been a slave all her life. I expected as much, for Grump had only been here a decade and she was in her early thirties, ten years my junior.

As to how she'd gotten here, she's been considered special since birth due to her remarkable skin color, a minor celebrity in her village. This had caused jealousy from girls and desire from boys. One of the latter, unable to attract her interest, had drugged and sold her to Grump's men in revenge, determined to put her in her place and show her that she wasn't special after all, just a property.

To some extent, he'd succeeded, but she'd been considered special here even before arrival, as word of her appearance preceded her. Grump had taken one look at her at the Golden Cruise welcome ceremony and *not* grabbed her by the pussy, directing others to keep their hands off her. He hadn't decided what to do with her, but until he did, no one was to violate her. She hadn't even been branded like the other girls, for to ruin that perfect, jet black skin was sacrilege. Jada wouldn't admit how long she'd been here, but it had been all light duties and not hard labor. Grump wanted something special for her, but there'd be no decision, until now, perhaps, when she'd been brought here for me.

"You haven't been made to, uh, be with, uh, anyone...?" I felt my face burn from the personal question.

"No. You would be the first. I do not know why. But it's been said you are a great man and have greatly honored and befriended His Majesty."

Now I wasn't sure what I was supposed to do with her. Grump obviously expected me to have sex with her. Would refusing be disobedience that might result in a visit from Mitch? I could always feign sickness. But then how would Jada feel? Rejected by the man she'd be given to after all this time? Would she care or be relieved? Or would Grump blame her for failing to please or interest me? Would he conclude she must not be that special after all? And what was to happen the next day? Did she go back to that life? Did I take her with me when I left? What was the plan here?

I wondered if she was a virgin and if this could be a problem. There was an old idea that, on the morning following a wedding, a proud husband would display the bloody sheets from a balcony to those below, having taken his wife's virginity. Was something similarly barbaric expected here? Would maids enter the room tomorrow and look for signs of lovemaking? At the least, Jada would have to spend the night. By now I had noticed Jada watching me silently, her face concerned, so I explained what I was thinking about this virginity thing and she put a comforting hand on my arm.

"I was examined by a doctor," she said. "They know I would not bleed any longer."

I admired her dancing around the detail, that her hymen had already broken, likely due to activity of some kind.

"I'm afraid you are right, though," she continued. "You must make love to me tonight for both our sakes, even if you do not want to."

I tried to smile as reassuringly as I could. "You don't need to worry about my interest. You already have it. My concern is that you should have an interest."

"Why?"

"Respect. It is what men do."

"Not all men. None here."

"This place is... different, as are these men."

"Maybe. Or maybe it is just you who is different."

I nodded a bit. "I am different from these men, it's true, but to me, they are not men. Men only have sex with women who want them, and women should only have sex with men they want."

"I am a slave. You do not need me to desire you."

"Yes, I do. I need you to desire me. I *want* you to."

"Why?" The coy smile about her lips suggested she knew the answer but wanted to see what else I'd say. I decided to humor her.

"Because you're a person, not a thing. Because you have an inner life. I can see it in your eyes, as silly as that may sound."

"It does not sound silly."

I nodded my thanks. Such a sentiment said in the U.C. would get me mocked by both sexes. "I wouldn't want to put out that light with my actions or words. Because if I just want to have sex, there are women here where that light has already gone out in them. You deserve better. So do I."

Her eyes seemed to shine more. "For a gentleman, you're very seductive."

I wasn't sure what to say but admitted, "You make me want to be honest."

"Why?"

"You ask that a lot," I observed.

"I like hearing what you think. Now tell me why I make you want to be honest with me. I like it, by the way."

I searched myself. "I'm not sure. I don't like the position you've been placed in. Now, or before tonight. It's not right. I feel terrible at the idea that I'm supposed to take advantage of you, that I'm to become part of a problem, a wound done to you."

"You have empathy. That is rare here except among the slaves."

"That's the way it should be."

"I learned to forget about how we want things to be and accepted how they are a long time ago."

"You shouldn't have to, and I'm not going to let that be the case when you're with me, as I can do something about that. People can make things be how they want."

Without resentment, she observed, "You can. I cannot."

"Tonight, you can. You are free until the morning."

She nodded but seemed unconvinced. "I appreciate what you are trying to do."

"But?"

Jada hesitated and then shrugged, looking away. "Nothing. You have shown me more kindness in a few minutes than I have seen in years." She stopped and then suddenly looked at me, several seconds of silent eye contact passing as I waited for her. "You are a good man."

We continued staring before her gaze fell to my lips. When her eyes met mine again, she smiled slightly and leaned toward me, planting a sweet kiss on my mouth. I felt a jolt of excitement.

Chapter 8 – "The Freedom Hunt"

Suddenly the Grump TV turned itself on by itself, grating music erupting amidst a slick production that flashed a light into the darkening room. Jada and I parted in surprise, the moment ruined. Sean Spacer gleefully appeared onscreen in a garish dancing outfit to announce that the District Road Race was about to begin, with eight contestants about to rack up points on their way to the finish line. Like many broadcasts, we were extolled to watch it, and I sensed that refusal would be discovered. I struggled to understand the rules and had felt Jada stiffen, so I asked her what was going on.

Once a month, the drivers left Grump Palace and hurtled into the four slave districts one location at a time. Each sportscar had been outfitted with spikes, guns, and other devices. The goal was for drivers to score points by running over whatever slaves happened to be out in the streets, killing them; those who didn't die were usually maimed, could no longer work as slaves, and were executed. Some people were worth more than others, such as the young, old, or just different. Those in the districts never knew when the race would happen for the obvious reason of remaining unprepared to escape. She didn't explain much more, for it became clear that, while she'd been protected from becoming a victim, she'd seen friends and others killed many times.

We watched from a couch with her sitting beside me so that we touched from hip to knee. I put an arm around her to ease her noticeable distress, my other hand taking hers as she leaned into me, often putting one hand to her mouth. She had never seen the race televised because there were no TVs in the districts. Spacer's delighted commentary as people were mowed down for entertainment was too much for her, and she trembled and cried beside me. Mercifully, the broadcast lasted less than an hour, each district terrorized for 15 minutes each, scores of people lying dead. We paid no more attention to the announced winner than we had to each act of wanton killing, as both of us averted our eyes and tried in vain to ignore Spacer's laughter.

The damn TV finally shut off. As we hadn't risen to turn on the lights, we now sat in darkness. Jada had stopped crying, but I continued to hold her, hearing myself repeatedly whisper that I was sorry for this horror she'd been forced to watch. She hadn't known about the point system or how the non-slaves viewed all of it. That it came as shock was obvious. She squeezed my hand, laying her head more on my shoulder. Moments later she turned to press her check into my chest, spending long moments there in the dark with me. To my surprise, she then kissed my neck, her lips lingering. I held back, feeling that sex after what we'd just witnessed seemed wholly inappropriate, but she repositioned herself and kissed me on the lips.

When she stopped, it was to rise to her feet with one hand in mine, clearly wanting me to go with her to the bed.

"Are you sure?" I asked, rising. "We don't have to."

"Yes, we do," she whispered. "And I want to. I've had enough death. Fill me with life, Max. Fill me with life."

She kissed me again, then excused herself for the bathroom. I made myself ready as well and waited for her to return, wondering at this turn of events. Could it be that in this horrible land, respect and kindness could still survive? With the lights off, I wanted to shield what was to happen, as if to protect it from prying eyes, and so when she returned to me, a nude, darker shadow moving against the blackness, I pulled her under the sheets and we made love.

Sometime later, as we lay in a spoon position, she asked if I was awake, and on learning that I was, chose to confide in me a secret. She'd been able to turn the jealousy often directed at her to an advantage, for the guards paid her less attention than others unless they thought she was in danger. They also did her favors, hoping to please Grump. These had allowed her to manipulate them into letting her do small things that she used for the benefit of the community, in secret.

And the greatest of these was the planning of an escape route they called the Underground Railroad, a series of tunnels to the west coast, dug each night and sometimes in the day. It had been happening since Grumpland was established, which told me how long she'd really been here. The route existed to smuggle slaves out of all the districts to safety if it ever seemed like Grumpland was indeed being attacked by the United Colonies or anyone else. Or if they somehow arranged for transport across the sea to Canada or beyond. Sometimes slaves went missing, or so Grump's guards thought, and it was believed that they had escaped into the Safari, but they had gone through the tunnels. She estimated that a thousand of them were out there somewhere in a small community, hidden in caves. If an opportunity arose for the slaves to escape, they would take it, finding their way to the sea, making their way to one of the many ports, stealing what boats they needed, and heading for the nearest land away from this place. When she wondered aloud how they'd get by Grump's wall, I told her it didn't exist, prompting a big kiss.

I also remembered being told that Grump had spies everywhere, even among the slaves. When I told her so, she replied with a smile that she already knew. Only a score of the earliest residents knew about the tunnels and understood how important secrecy was. She wouldn't tell me how they kept others from knowing about it, but I accepted that she had it under control or else it would've long since been shut down.

We fell asleep soon after.

In the morning, I woke to the delight of Jada pressed into my side, her open eyes already on me. We shared a smile and kiss before agreeing to meet again soon. She excused herself and left my rooms, just as the TV screen in the bedroom turned on by itself. The usual announcements and Grump praise blared forth, the harsh messages scattering the sweet atmosphere of lovemaking that had filled the room. I tried to get away by going into the bathroom, but the TV there turned on, too, the omnipresent Grump propaganda only drowned out by the sound of my pee falling onto Hillary Minton's visage.

After a shower, I found a camouflage outfit laid out for me on the bed, which had been changed with fresh linens. A hearty breakfast lay on a table and I snacked in between putting on the cargo pants, socks, boots, t-shirt, and a button-up flannel. I tucked the hat into a pocket and headed for the door. On opening it, I found Svetlana waiting for me in a similar outfit, though hers was form-fitting and alluring, a plunging neckline tempting the eye.

"I hope you ate your fill," she remarked, leading me down the hall. "We have a big day."

"Tell me, is everyone required to watch the hunt?"

"Of course. Even the slaves in the districts."

That meant guarding my reactions. I'd have to mimic those around me to blend in and save my horrified looks for later.

As we traveled to the Safari, Svetlana filled me in on what to expect. An avid hunter, I initially felt no need of her explanations, but she assured me this hunt was unlike any I'd ever experienced, and based on her account, it was true. The highlight was, of course, the hunting of the captured pilot, Barry. He had been set loose the night before with some small manner of provisions to ensure he survived the night. Hunting someone already dead offered no sport. He'd also been healed from the minor wounds suffered in his plane crash. We were to expect a lively hunt. As to whether he'd been armed or not, Svetlana assured me that nothing, and no one, in the Safari had a weapon unless they'd fashioned one themselves, and that such crude devices were no match for our state-of-the-art armament.

We arrived at a sleek but brutish facility that towered over us, glass, steel, and granite looming menacingly. Like all buildings here, Grump's name was emblazoned across it. Lookouts high atop the twin towers were visible from below and were primed with first-rate telescopes and binoculars to scan for good hunting areas, based on what prey they saw. The Safari stretched for untold miles and was fenced in all around to prevent escape. I'd seen the grounds from the palace, to which it was adjacent so that Inner Party members with the right skills could use sniper rifles to murder people from the comfort of their suites.

My guide was coy about what manner of creatures we'd find there beside Barry. I felt the excitement of the others around me. They badly wanted my fellow Amnesian to be hunted and murdered for sport. It reminded me of my own peril, for should I displease the emperor in any way, I might find myself the next prey. I made a mental note to keep tabs on everything I saw in case I might need it for my own survival.

Svetlana led me through various halls and doorways to a room with all manner of guns and other gadgets I couldn't discern the purpose of. She took various items and armed both me and herself. I received a handgun, an automatic rifle, a whip, elastic ties for handcuffing people, a wicked-looking knife, and a stun gun. Several extra bullet magazines were strapped to me or placed in pockets. Svetlana armed herself with several strange-looking weapons and spare battery packs, but nothing as ordinary as me, which prompted me to ask about the differences.

"Well comrade," she began, "since you're new here and haven't had proper weapons training, I'm only outfitting you with traditional weapons. But I've been trained in all the gadgets we have and plan to use them effectively! You haven't really lived until you've liquified someone with a plasma rifle."

I nodded at the silver and blue weapon she hoisted. "I'll take your word for it."

"Oh, don't pout!" she teased. "I'll arrange for some training tomorrow if you'd like."

"I would love that, thank you."

She squeezed my ass and led me through a few more rooms before we arrived in a TV studio, where a multitude of people were preparing for a broadcast that we were apparently intended to join. A sexually dressed blonde forced me into a seat and applied makeup while Svetlana received the same from a brunette. Once finished, we moved to another room to join men outfitted just like us. Then Emperor Grump strode in with a sinister-looking, muscle-bound man in combat fatigues. He wore a nasty scar across his face from forehead to the opposite cheek. Everything about him oozed menace and violence, yet capability. I feared him instantly.

Grump turned to me and gestured at him. "This is Zarof, Master of the Hunt. He'll be our guide. He's a good man from Ukraine, our ally."

Zarof looked at me coldly. I nodded a greeting he didn't return.

We gathered on a platform with a TV camera pointed at us. Svetlana instructed me in a suitable hunter's pose where I assumed a fierce expression and held my weapon aloft. Others took a variety of stances as a well-produced, splashy intro that showed various scenes from past hunts, all with the emperor bringing down the prey personally. Then the camera rolled, and Grump addressed the nation.

"Dear citizens," he began, "today we begin this month's Freedom Hunt, where the objects of our pursuit gains their freedom from slavery, to join us as rightful citizens if they survive until midnight. But as you know, no one has ever done it. And how could they with me, the greatest hunter in the world, after them? As usual, we've chosen two tributes from each of the four districts, and this morning, they were let loose into the Safari with ample supplies and weapons to defend themselves with.

"And this hunt is special. Very special. One of the animals is the worst, most vile creature out there. And just a savage. It's a black man, a pilot, who soared over our empire with evil intentions to bomb all us out of existence. He's a citizen of the Treasonous United Colonies."

"Hail Grump!" shouted everyone present, from cameramen to those on the platform, including myself.

"We will hunt him down most of all," Grump continued, "and I will personally deliver the kill shot. Only I am strong enough to take him down. Only I can protect you. Only I can make all your dreams come true, for I am the Chosen One."

After this dramatic ending, he stopped speaking and assumed an expression like the condescending sculpture of himself on Mt. Grumpmore. Then a director yelled "Cut!" and everyone relaxed.

"You two are with me," said Grump, indicating me and Svetlana. I had expected no less and fell in beside him as we moved toward a rugged, all-terrain truck with open sides. It was armed with various space-age weaponry, from canons to guns and things I couldn't even describe. I doubted I had long before I found out what the weapons did to people.

A producer announced that we were ready to begin, and Grump Hunter One, as I learned it was dubbed, rolled toward bay doors that opened into the bright morning sunlight, with two other vehicles, far less weaponized, following. Two cameramen were aboard our vehicle as we rumbled out into Grump Safari and the Freedom Hunt had begun. A screen near the vehicle's front acted like radar, with multiple blinking lights indicating the location of various targets. We appeared to be following a pair of them that had stuck close together.

"Probably from the same district," Svetlana mused beside me.

"Why are there two chosen from a district?"

"Male and female, except for the gays. There the combination changes all the time. Sometimes it's two guys, or two girls, or one gay and one lesbian. One time it was two bisexuals. The emperor's favorites are transsexuals. He always makes them go naked so they can't hide what they really are."

"Then how does he know what he's killing?"

"Oh, everyone has a specific brand they wear so we can identify the corpse. Blacks get the continent Africa branded on them. Mexicans get a maraca. Muslims get the crescent moon and star. Gays get their little rainbow flag. That reminds me, captured Democrats get branded, too, with a donkey."

"Of course."

The nearest targets were close and Zarof indicated it was time to get out and go on foot. He led the way with Grump right beside him. Trees and brush dotted the otherwise rocky landscape. It seemed apparent that our prey was hiding behind some of them. Zarof checked the scanner in one hand and then motioned at a copse of pine trees. Grump trained his machine gun and fired into the boughs, causing a hail of leaves to dislodge. Suddenly a tall, naked Indian woman ran from them into the open, a naked man following and begging her to return. He looked at us with wide eyes before racing after her.

Grump grinned at me. "Now comes the fun part."

We hopped back into Hunter One and took off after the two Muslims, but we moved slowly, letting them easily stay ahead of us as Grump or others fired shots to one side or the other, herding them. I wondered if they had a plan or were just toying with the tributes. The answer proved to be both. Before long, they'd been chased into a narrow valley with only one way out, and we blocked it. We stopped to pursue on foot.

"Bring the rack, comrades," said Grump over one shoulder.

To my raised eyebrow, Svetlana just smiled and patted my rump on her way past me.

"Tell me," I began, following, "you said the gays are naked. I thought you meant only them, but these two are naked. Why?"

"The emperor is a great admirer of the female body and he dislikes the way Muslim women are all covered up, so he makes them go without. On the first few hunts, the males always gave the females some of their clothing, so now they go naked, too. Problem solved."

"I see."

We advanced slowly and soon found the pair huddled against a cliff face, panting, dusty, and sweating despite the cold. The woman tried to hide her nakedness, but Grump was having none of that. He barked for the rack and a metal frame was brought forward and assembled. One of Zarof's men apprehended first the woman and then the man, neither of whom fought much, horrified resignation in their eyes. In short order, both were tied to the rack, their arms above the heads and spread wide, like their legs. From a distance, each looked like a human X. The positioning offered no modesty. Grump approached the woman but gestured carelessly at the man's genitals.

"Cut that off," he said. "No one wants to see that."

Zarof stepped forward and with a smooth swing of his knife, emasculated the man, who screamed as his penis and testicles fell into the dust. Zarof picked them up and tossed them onto a small electric grill that I hadn't noticed someone setting up. The flesh crackled as they burned. He took a hot poker from the grill, approached the man, and jammed it into the wound. The man's hideous screaming made me wince.

"Can't have you bleeding to death on us," said a grinning Zarof, pulling the poker away from the cauterized wound.

Grump stood before the woman, grabbing her here, there, and everywhere, commenting on just how lovely each part of her body was. He suggested everyone present take a turn enjoying her and other crude remarks, which he labeled "locker room talk." Then he observed that they didn't have time for any extra fun with her, which was a pity. He stepped away and came up beside me, hefting a rock.

"You want the first shot?"

I looked at the fist-sized stone he offered me. "Sire?"

He turned back to look at the tributes and said conversationally. "You know, I really don't appreciate the way people say I have no appreciation for other cultures. You see, Muslims are big on stoning people to death for crimes, so that's what we do with them here. Doesn't that seem respectful of their shitty culture? Of course, it does. Of course, it does. Besides, bullets are too good for them. They're savages. Just look at them."

I nodded.

"Sometimes we tie explosives to them and do it that way. Cause you know they're all terrorists, right? That's how they bomb places. Makes quite a mess, but we're out here where it doesn't matter." He hefted the rock again and turned to me. "Would you like the honor of the first stone?"

"I'm flattered, Your Majesty, but the honor should be yours."

"I agree. It should be." He moved closer to the victims and threw the first rock at the male, missing, so he picked up another and threw it with the same result. Then he looked back and barked a short laugh. "The editors will fix that. Zarof!"

The master of the hunt hurled a rock that struck the man in the face, then stepped back to form a line with others in our group. Each began hurling stones at the Muslims. I stood staring at the bloody cuts appearing one by one on their bodies, their screams sometimes interrupted by a blow to the face, throat, or chest. Svetlana nudged me before throwing a rock and I realized I hadn't participated, so I began to do so.

At first, I missed on purpose, but then Grump asked, "Weren't you a baseball pitcher in high school?"

Startled that he knew this, I quickly thought of a lie. "Yes, sire. Just out of practice."

"Well get closer. Can't have you missing. You're worse than me!"

My stomach knotted. Watching others in their cruelty was quite different from doing it myself. The awfulness of being here was ratcheting up. Was I being indoctrinated in the evil here? What would be left of my morality, my soul, after two weeks of this? I had no time for such pondering and stepped closer. I threw a stone and struck the man in the stomach. Suddenly I realized the greatest act I could do was to kill them quickly.

Acting as though I was overcome with passion, I grabbed a head-sized rock and ran forward, screaming incoherently as I bashed the woman over the head with it. Her head caved in and death was easy to see. Then I turned and did the same to the man, striking repeatedly, blooding splattering all over me. The act triggered the growing rage about all I had seen, and I could finally stop pretending and let it out. If a maniacal look appeared on my face, it wasn't feigned. I stood breathing heavily as I turned back toward the others, choking back bile. I had just murdered two people.

Grump stood beaming, like a proud father, and the others began clapping and hollering.

"Thataboy!" Grump shouted. "Thataboy!"

I dropped the rock to my feet and walked back toward the truck, having no need to fake how I trembled. Svetlana grabbed me and planted a deep kiss on me. Under other circumstances, I would've welcomed it, but I now used it to close my eyes and hide my face until she pulled away.

The men removed the bodies, left them in the dirt, and disassembled the frame, clambering back into Grump One as we went in search of the other tributes. As we went, I saw above us some winged humanoids, a pack of a dozen, flying toward where we... where I had killed the Muslims. I did a doubletake, for such a creature, which Svetlana called "bat kids," could not be real. They were the size of children, wearing light clothing and having a leathery membrane from wrist to shoulder. As I watched, Svetlana trained her rifle at one and fired. A blue bolt of light struck and surrounded one. It curled into a ball and fell writhing to the ground as the others around it scattered.

"Scavengers," Grump announced to me. "They'll be feeding on the corpses in a few minutes. Never hurts to thin their numbers. That was a good shot."

"Thank you, Your Majesty," replied my guide.

We continued into the wilderness for thirty minutes, all signs of civilization slowly disappearing behind us, though the pyramid could be seen from everywhere. Along the way, we saw other animals that defied explanation, but most heard us coming and fled before we reached them. We came across a black-furred puma that stood upright and walked like a graceful human, so much so that I wondered if it were a person in a costume. Later, what looked to be a polar bear slid into the water, but it had no snout and instead had a head like a human; it swam freestyle like one, too. In another instance, we saw several male, black minotaurs, their bull-like heads alertly following our vehicle until we turned toward them, and they ran into a cave; Svetlana said it went for miles so that it was hard to find them inside.

A pack of dogs was seen awkwardly loping ahead of us until we came closer, whereupon they stopped and hid behind bushes. I had stared at the unnatural gait, wondering what ailed them, but upon nearing, it became apparent that each had human-like legs, arms, feet, and hands that were likely causing it. Thick fur covered most of them, a bushy tail hung from behind, and above a canine snout were eyes that seemed disturbingly human and yet half-crazed. Zarof fired into the air and the dog-men scattered, running in their bizarre way as Grump singled out one and we pursued in Hunter One. I thought he'd use a gun to kill it, but the car's driver simply mowed it down, a human-like yelp sounding from below us as we bounced over the body. It lay twitching behind us as we continued, Grump laughing all the while.

"Never seen their like, have you?" Grump beamed at me, gloating. "These savages only exist here. You'll never guess where they come from."

"I can't imagine," I admitted.

"Svetlana," he began. "Why don't you show Max to the White Utopia Building after the hunt?"

"My pleasure, Your Majesty."

"And when you're done, show him the Golden Armory, as well. I know he's wondering where these great devices come from."

Minutes later, Zarof motioned to stop the car and we exited near a stand of trees that he led us into. He seemed to sense that something was here. I glanced around nervously. Maybe if he killed one of these creatures, I could get a good look at it.

After several minutes of quietly stepping around twigs and rocks, Zarof motioned us to be quiet, so we waited as he crept forward without us. He reached a tree and peered forward and down for several moments before motioning us forward. We moved quietly, wondering what was amiss, and soon joined the hunt master at a ravine. At the bottom, among the dried-out trails, lay a scene of horror.

A pink beast lay on its back, sightless, human eyes staring past us above a pig-like snout. Its throat had been savagely torn out. Four hooves stood in the air but little else could be seen due to another creature above it. We could only see the human-like back, buttocks, and legs as it crouched over the pig-man, low growls of satisfaction and contentment louder than the slurping sounds we heard. It appeared to be devouring the pig-man's belly, rooting through for precious organs. A bald head moved up and down, sometimes shaking vigorously as if trying to tear through flesh and sinew with what I presumed were razor-sharp teeth. Like all the beasts we'd seen, I couldn't help but wonder what madness had led to this one's existence.

To my surprise, Emperor Grump laughed beside me and patted my shoulder. "Steve!" he called out, beginning to climb down toward the scene "Steve, it's us! Don't bite!"

Dread overcoming me, I followed him and Zarof, who had his gun carefully cocked, unlike His Majesty. As we neared the predator, it suddenly stopped, head whipping in our direction. I took an involuntary step back. Its eyes were dilated and wild. Blood drenched its entire face. From its mouth hung entrails that it slurped between pointed teeth. I wasn't expecting the beast to speak, and only when it did could I recognize it at last.

"Master," it snarled.

I recoiled. "Stephen Killer?"

Chapter 9 – "Dr. Josef Morjekstein"

"Yep." Grump beamed. "I knew he had a killer instinct when we met. He's very tough on immigrants. Very tough. You can't be weak."

"Why is he naked?" I asked.

"Dunno. Never got a good answer to that myself."

Svetlana suggested, "Maybe it's the animal nature we're seeing."

Grump scratched his jowls. "Yeah, that could be it." We stood and watched as Killer went back to his feast and Grump finally turned back to me, seeming resigned. "I guess we should let him finish. We'll see you back at the palace tonight, okay Steve?"

For a response, Killer tore a foreleg off the victim and tossed it to Grump's feet.

"Good boy! Good boy!" Grump smirked at me. "They say a dog is man's best friend, but I wonder. He practically lives out here, you know. Hard to find him when you want him. We leave a bowl of immigrant blood out on the back porch if we really need to talk to him."

We headed back to Hunter One and I risked one last glance back at the still-feeding human, who seemed more a beast than anything else we'd encountered. The hunger I saw in his ferocious eyes as they locked on to me sent a chill down my spine.

We continued in pursuit of the next targets. There were six tributes left, plus the main quarry, Barry. He'd been outfitted with a tracker, too, deep in his skin like the others so that he'd never get it out. From the radar, we couldn't tell who he was because there were two dots staying together in one area, two more in another, and the remaining three targets had separated, which suggested one pair of tributes had split up. The question was which pair, and which of the single blips was Barry?

We began closing in on the nearest pair, who turned out to be from the gay district. This caused Grump to cheerfully command the grill to be fired up. I suspected why and soon got confirmation when, from the still moving Hunter One, the running pair were shot in the back by some sort of stunning weapon that made them fall senseless to the ground. Zarof promptly pulled from the truck another metal restraining contraption, this one being two vertical poles to which the dazed were tied with their hands above the heads. Svetlana told me the homosexuals were usually killed by firing squad this way, and that was precisely how Grump executed them with some sort of plasma gun that vaporized them.

"Nothing should be left of those sickos," Grump said. "We don't even want the bat kids to eat these. They might turn all gay, too. Better that no sign of them remain."

We clambered back into the truck and continued, picking up the pace now that lunchtime was nearing and we were miles into the Safari. Grump indicated we should go after one of the lone targets and we spent an hour chasing after. It proved to be the Latino male. He scampered over rock outcroppings with such an impressive frenzy that had Grump comparing his climbing skills to that of a monkey. He mused that no wall could keep out such an animal. He began firing various guns at the tribute. One cannon blasted a huge chunk of stone to dust. Another sent out a horizontal beam of blue light that cut trees in half, but the sound of timber falling alerted the intended victim, who looked back, saw this, and dove to the ground before running once more. A grenade launcher fired by Zarof blasted chunks of earth from the ground, one of them striking close enough to launch the man into the sky. He landed hard and didn't move. Grump carefully aimed his rifle, looking for signs of life, and when the man stirred, Grump fired a shot that missed. His next bullet struck a leg, then missed again as the man began dragging himself across the ground for cover.

"They never give up, these damn Latinos," said Grump. "They're like vermin."

Hunter One drove up near the man and stopped. The man began begging for his life, but Grump just remarked to us that it was lunchtime. I hadn't expected what happened next. From the truck's compartments, the men pulled out a folding metal table and set it up on a flat area of low grass not ten feet from the dying man. Then they covered it with a rich tablecloth. Four padded chairs were quickly assembled, one for His Majesty, Svetlana, Zarof, and myself. Men set the table with fine china, sterling silver, and crystal goblets before filling them with a dark, fizzing soda that tasted like Diet Coke. We then dined on McGrump Big Dons, fish fillet sandwiches, and fries. For dessert, we enjoyed cherry vanilla ice cream on cones. Emperor Grump repeatedly licked this while the man bled to death feet from him.

"Would you like a last meal?" a grinning Grump asked him.

"Beg your pardon, sire," began Zarof, "but the tributes might be considered to have already received one in the form of their rations. Perhaps this would be more than the creatures deserve."

Grump considered. "It would be a waste anyway, wouldn't it? Animals." He pulled out a handgun and shot the man in the head, then licked his ice cream cone a few more times before dropping the rest next to the corpse and putting the gun away. He started back for Hunter One and sat patiently while everything was put away and we started for another pair of tributes. This time, we knew who they were because only the black slaves remained as a pair that had stayed together; somewhere out there was the Latino woman, and Barry.

We soon corralled the black slaves as Zarof hoisted a bola and began twirling it above his head. He stood on a platform above the rear wheels. The metal balls began whirring overhead. As we neared the woman, Zarof expertly threw it at her legs, around which they swiftly wrapped, bringing her to the ground. We took off after the man and Zarof repeated the feat on the first try once more. Then we stopped and he attached a cable to the man's bola before hopping back into Hunter One. Dragging him behind us, we drove a short way to the woman, whose bola he also attached to the cable. Zarof climbed back in and donned a seatbelt. Hunter One began rolling.

"They're not worth the trouble of getting out of the truck," Svetlana assured me, smiling and looking back. I saw that both tributes were slowly being dragged behind us, but as the vehicle picked up speed, this changed. At first, I thought the driver avoided low rocks and other debris to avoid causing unnecessary pain, but he was only prolonging their deaths, which also explained the relatively sedate pace at which we moved. Finally, Grump announced that he was bored and looking forward to watching his favorite TV shows soon, so the driver gunned it and behind us, the bodies bounced mercilessly across the earth. We never even slowed when they had died, for the bodies slowly dismembered and before long, we were only dragging the bolas themselves. Zarof flicked on the winch and the cable to which they were attached neatly coiled up in place as before.

Two single blips remained on the radar and we pursued the nearest one, which proved to be the Latino woman. Grump, being in a hurry now, simply sprayed her with machine-gun fire, bringing her down from behind. He continued firing into her body until it was clear she'd expired. We continued.

A short while later, Zarof motioned to stop. We were many miles into the Safari now and he'd seen smoke from among the trees. We left Hunter One behind and crept through the woods to a strange scene before us. A group of several dozen humanoids was tending to tents, cooking fires, or each other, though most were pacing around among the trees, seemingly muttering to themselves. We weren't close enough to overhear. All of them wore tattered robes or mismatched outfits, each with holes and bloodstains. Many were barefoot, bare-chested, or even fully nude, which made it easy to see that every last one of them had white skin with what looked like extensive stitching. In fact, their bodies gave an impression of having been stitched together, as if body parts had been sewn to make them. But they were all human at least.

Suddenly one of them saw us watching and screamed. The others whirled toward us amidst an outcry of terror. They ran to stand close together. I could see them trembling as Emperor Grump and the hunters slowly moved toward them, blocking any escape.

"What are these?" I asked, having stifled such questions all day but no longer able to contain myself.

Zarof answered. "More of Karson's, no doubt."

"Karson?"

Ignoring my question, Grump said, "Not much fun to kill them, as they aren't even trying to get away. Must not be very smart. Probably can't even talk."

One of the male creatures stepped forward only to have a female put a restraining hand on him. "Granger, no. Please," she pleaded.

"It's okay, Millie," he whispered. With a kindly smile toward her, he gently removed her hand and took two steps toward us until Grump's hunters pointed various devices at him.

"Your Majesty," he began in a deep voice, hands raised. The hunters lowered their weapons. "Please allow us to remain. We don't bother anyone here or the others in the Safari. We have hidden here for many years and never disturbed anyone or your hunts."

Grump looked down his nose at Granger. "Then what is it that you do here? What was that muttering to yourself we heard? All of you were doing it. Sounded like a plot against me."

"No! Not us, sire! We would never harm you, Your Benevolence."

"Then what were you saying?" Grump seemed imperious. I'd never seen the emperor look more menacing.

Granger hesitated, but a little girl, no more than six, stepped forward. Like all of them, her face appeared stitched together. "Books, sire. We were reciting books."

"Lakisha, no!" the woman cried, pulling the girl back as the hunters raised their weapons once more, as if a deadly threat had been made against them.

Grump had recoiled. "Books! I banned those! How do you have books?" After a moment of frozen horror, he gestured at the tents and several hunters began violently tearing them apart in a search for the illicit materials.

Granger replied, "We don't, sire. None of us have a book. Please, we are peaceful."

"I'm not." Grump stood fuming as the camp was torn apart, but after five minutes, nothing had been found. Zarof came forward.

"If I may, Your Majesty? I think I know what's happened here. They have memorized books and are reciting them to themselves to avoid forgetting."

Grump's expression became haughtier, if that were possible. "So. So it *is* a plot against me."

"No, sire!" Granger pleaded, face aghast. He dropped to his knees in submission and the others followed suit.

"Should we get the firemen?" Zarof asked.

"Firemen?" I asked. I didn't see any fire needing to be put out.

Grump considered. "Well, they appear to have memorized books, and what do we do with those?"

"Burn them!"

"Books are evil!"

"They're a hoax!"

"Fake news!"

Grump smiled in satisfaction as the hunters angrily denounced the medium. "Precisely. Call them in."

At this, a cry of despair went up from the bibliophiles, who began to huddle together with much wailing and gnashing of teeth. This went on for several moments while Zarof spoke over the radio to someone. Then Grump indicated everyone be silent. Only the pitiful moans of the book lovers rent the still air.

"I've changed my mind," he said. At this, tears of relief poured down the stitched faces of the creatures. "We won't burn you. Not here. Not today." He paused for emphasis and then said triumphantly. "We'll burn you alive at the next Hillary Fest!"

The shout of enthusiasm from the hunters nearly drowned out the cries of terror from the sacrifices, some of whom fainted. They were easy to bind before we left them behind, a few hunters remaining to watch over them as they waited for a helicopter to arrive. As we drove on, he remarked that this gave new meaning to "catch and kill."

Grump grew more excited at the prospect of killing Barry, for he wanted to make a great show of finally killing Osama. We tracked him to a forest that had enough underbrush that we couldn't enter. Worse, the ground rose sharply to a set of small peaks in the middle. I'd seen it in the distance and hadn't imagined that anyone could reach it, but this was a soldier we were pursuing. As we exited Hunter One on foot, taking a healthy supply of weapons with us, Zarof reminded us that, unlike the tributes, the prey was a trained killer and we needed to be on guard. Some of the hunters went ahead of us and we began to spread out. I stayed close to the heart of the hunting party: Grump, Zarof, and Svetlana.

We hadn't gone far into the forest when the slope began to rise. Zarof's men ahead of indicated that Barry's tracks led farther in and likely up one of the peaks. Suddenly a scream split the air and men rushed forward to a grizzly scene. A hunter stood gasping in pain, his legs impaled by several wooden stakes that were attached to a long branch, which had whipped around when he'd sprung Barry's trap. Zarof grinned, seeming pleased to have a real hunt. Neither he or Grump gave the wounded man another thought as we continued following others, who had gone farther up the trail.

Just minutes later, another man began firing a gun into the woods to one side. On seeing a figure in a coat, the others began shooting, too, until the master of the hunt yelled at them to stop. It was a decoy... Barry having put his coat onto a cross-shaped pair of branches he'd fashioned for the purpose. As we continued, the traps and decoys did as well, but none claimed a life. It couldn't be an accident. The prey we hunted clearly had survivalist skills we lacked. I began to hang back from the group, afraid to be maimed. Seeing this, Svetlana rolled her eyes at me and continued. I wondered if it was too late to go back to Hunter One. And that's when I realized that, were I Barry, I'd lure the hunters up to the peaks and steal the mostly unguarded vehicle; we'd left only one man with it. By the time this occurred to me, the others had stepped away too far for me to warn them without yelling and giving away our position, so I turned around and started back.

Hardly two minutes had passed when a shadow leapt at me from the bushes and pinned me to a tree, one hand over my mouth as cold eyes stared into mine. I felt the sharp point of a weapon against my throat.

"Don't make a sound," Barry commanded in a fierce whisper. "Understand?" I nodded mutely and after more silent glaring, he pulled his hand away.

"What are you going to do?" I whispered.

"I recognize you," he said, ignoring my question. "I know you. You're not one of these monsters. You're from the U.C., too."

"That's right."

"What are you doing here? You're the one who's been sending them here."

I licked my suddenly dry lips. "I didn't know what it's really like here and regret every minute of it."

He pressed the sharp object into my throat painfully. "Then help me get off this island. Give me something. What haven't I seen in my mission briefs about this place that you have since you've been here? Something that can help me escape."

I racked my brain to and then remembered what Jada told me that morning. "The districts."

"What about them?"

"Get to District One, the black one. They have an Underground Railroad where they hide slaves. You can disappear there until you find a way off the island."

"How do I know you're telling me the truth?"

"You don't. There's a resistance here. Ask for Ebony Girl, her real name is Jada, and tell them Max sent you. She'll know."

We heard the sound of men coming in our direction, backtracking. He let me go and clasped my hand.

"Thank you. Give that bastard a message for me."

"What?"

"Don't push it. Don't push it or I'll give you a war you won't believe."

I nodded but observed, "You're doing some pushing on your own now."

"They drew first blood, not me. Sorry about this," he said, and before I could ask what he meant, he punched me hard in the jaw and I fell to the ground. Barry turned away and made his way down the trail toward Hunter One. I hesitated, not knowing what to do. I didn't want to be stranded out here with everyone. I couldn't go with him. But then I heard people rushing toward me and realized he'd known they were coming and given me cover.

Svetlana stopped to help me up as the rest of the hunting party chased after their prey. Unfortunately for Barry, Hunter One was parked far enough from the woods that he was still in the open and running for it when we burst from the trees. Everyone opened fire, which drew the attention of the lone guard we'd left behind. He hopped behind a heat cannon and aimed it Barry, who kept running at him. With a horrible whirring sound, the weapon revved up and fired a vertical, hollow circle of red light that passed over Barry, who turned to ash and drifted into the sky on the breeze. Except for a small pile of grey on the ground, there was no sign he'd ever existed.

The Freedom Hunt was over.

I thought we'd drive back but Grump didn't want to waste so much time, so two helicopters arrived – one for him and one for Svetlana and me. She brought me to a facility on the eastern shore, "because dawn should shine on this place where our White Utopia, a new beginning, will arise," she said. I gazed in wonder at the steel and glass structure below. Unlike others on the island, it lacked a brooding, hulking menace and instead seem open and welcoming. It was oval with multiple layers of folded steel and glass, like a flower. In the middle were two smooth openings, the upper one spraying a fountain of golden water into the air. Our craft began to lower toward the lower hole, a kind of landing pad waiting down within the glistening tunnel, when I realized that the White Utopia Building was shaped like a vulva. Seeing my expression, Svetlana laid a firm hand on my thigh.

"It is a place of birth after all," she observed.

On landing, I somehow sensed which of two tunnels to take and led her onward. We passed by rooms whose purpose I could not discern, though each appeared medical in nature. Beds with restraints dominated them, always surrounded by unknown machines of white and steel, often with tubes and wires hanging haphazardly. A few technicians in white lab coats were cleaning various facilities and apparatuses, saying little as our footsteps rang on the polished stone floors. Finally, we arrived at a room with two glass doors that my guide led me through.

Before us lay a large room with multiple, adjacent alcoves along the walls, each opening covered by hanging plastic or fabrics to obscure what lay beyond. Various freezers, refrigerators, cabinets, and wheeled machinery lined the walls or dotted the floor. In the center lay several operating tables, the requisite bright lights hanging above, but only one was occupied, by something I could not see, and a man that appeared to be a surgeon of some kind stood in a white robe with his back to me. At the sound of our steps, he turned around and, with bloody fingers, pulled down the mask over his face to reveal a grey beard on a distinguished black face. I recognized him, though I had not seen him in years.

"You remember Dr. Benji Karson, comrade," Svetlana began, leading me forward, "the former U.C. Secretary of Housing and Urban Development. He is our Angel of Life, the Bringer of the Foretold Age, when white people will rule the world once more."

I tried to hide my surprise that a blank man was helping bring about the White Utopia, especially this one. He had publicly disapproved of Grump as a candidate for president, but then fell silent after Grump was elected. Perhaps this was nothing more than a progression to its natural conclusion?

Karson smiled warmly and peeled off the bloody gloves, dropping them in a wastebasket as he advanced. His surgeon's smock had been fastened tightly at the neck. "Leave us," he commanded my guide, and Svetlana bowed before departing. He then shook my hand. "Max Worth. I'm so pleased you're here."

"Thank you, Dr. Karson. They didn't tell me what kind of work you're doing. I think they wanted it to be a surprise by you showing me firsthand."

"Gladly! I understand you just came from the Safari."

"I did."

"What did you think?"

I wasn't sure how to respond. "I've never seen people hunted for sport before. They certainly proved a challenge."

"Yes, but what about my creations? The animals?"

My eyebrows rose. "You created them? What do you mean? I thought maybe they were some indigenous species I'd never seen before."

He laughed. "Not at all. Come let me show you. I'm working on another right now."

Karson led me to the table where he'd been working under bright lights. At first glance, what looked like a large puma lay spread on the table, bound arm and leg to the steel frame. Whiskers protruded from its feline muzzle, which curled back in a sneer on seeing the doctor, baring sharp teeth. A tail trembled between its legs. But as I gazed at its eyes, I saw they were not the irises of a cat but that of a human. And the intelligence in them far surpassed that of any feline. Its gaze met mine, a look of desperation passing over its features before the doctor leaned toward it and the animal growled low and deep.

"Magnificent, isn't she?" Karson asked, beaming.

"Yes. But what is it?"

"Hard to say. A better question would be, what is it becoming? I would venture to say it's becoming its natural state. That of an animal. That's the whole point, of course. Would you believe that this was once a black human female in her early 20s?"

I could not hide my surprise. Surely, he was kidding. "But...How?"

"Oh, it's too complicated to explain my methods. Besides, can't have you steal my work and the Nobel Prize I'll surely be awarded. The emperor has long stated that blacks, Latinos, and other non-white are nothing more than savages, animals. And he was right! With a little proper prodding, I've been able to turn thousands of them into their natural state, which is inferior to whites. The primitive beast lurks within." He injected the snarling beast with a needle, and it fell silent, eyes closing. It was apparently asleep now.

I stared at the pitiful creature, questions swirling, but one stood out above the others. "I'm afraid I have to ask a delicate question."

"By all means."

I paused, then sighed. "I mean no offense, but how is it that a black man has these attitudes about his own race? Don't you fear that, when you perfect these techniques, Emperor Grump will use them upon yourself?"

He laughed uproariously, clapping me on the shoulder. At least I had not offended him.

"An excellent question indeed, comrade, but I have a solution to that very problem." He led me to a refrigerator and pulled out a phial of blood-red liquid. Pulling off the stopper, he sniffed it languidly and then made a toasting motion to me, though I had nothing to imbibe. Then he downed a mouthful in one eager gulp.

He replaced the stopper and glass before gazing at me with a smirk. His demeanor suggested something was afoot. Suddenly, his fingers began to shorten as his hands shrunk. His belly swelled. Atop his balding head, first a tuft of golden hair appeared, then more sprouted wildly before settling into a combover. But worst of all was his skin, which turned from brown to a mottled grey, then white, and finally a sickly orange. His expression had settled into one of unimpressed disdain. It was only then that I realized with a start that he'd nearly turned into the emperor himself!

"It's not superficial," Karson advised me. "The potion turns me into a white man through to my bones. No trace of black DNA left at all. Trust me. I've checked. I also made my own addition to the formula. Everyone who consumes it will feel an overwhelming desire for overpriced and unnecessary luxury furniture."

I stopped myself from gaping. "How long does it last?"

"Several hours, but this is increasing. It seems that the more I take it, the more effective it is. Just last week, to my delight, I actually woke up as my white self without having taken the potion! This suggests that, before long, I won't even need it and will be permanently white. This exceeds my wildest dreams!"

"Do you feel superior once you've transformed?"

He chuckled. "Of course. White people *are* superior. If Emperor Grump has taught me anything, it is this."

"Do you have enough to transform others? That way you wouldn't need to turn them into animals." This seemed less cruel and a lesser evil, though both possibilities were appalling.

Karson rolled his eyes. "Well, for starters, they *are* animals, not humans, as my lord has said, but what would we hunt on the Safari?"

Trying not to offend him, I suggested, "Real animals?"

"These *are* real animals. It's just easier to see that when I'm finished with them. They're actually better than other animals because they do have a modicum of intelligence and that makes the hunts so much better."

"I suppose I hadn't thought of that."

"Besides, I don't have enough of the potion anyway."

"Why not make more?"

"I've tried. Something is amiss. I've tried to recreate it a thousand times to no avail. At first, I thought I had done a step incorrectly, or in the wrong order. Maybe I had missed an ingredient or used the wrong amount. But no, I have the recipe written down and followed it exactly."

"Then what?"

"Well, I next thought that one of the ingredients was tainted, so I kept ordering more and from different places. I went through them one by one. Eventually, I reached the obvious conclusion. It wasn't the new ingredients that were tainted, but one from the original batch. I don't know which or from where it came. There's nothing I can do." He tapped the phial. "This is all that is left."

Trying to sound like I meant it, I said, "A terrible predicament."

"I must ask you not to tell the emperor there is no more."

"He knows about this?" I didn't know why this surprised me at first, but I realized it was obvious he'd know. What Karson said next came as no revelation.

"Of course. It was his idea. It's all part of his master plan to raise the Master Race to the height of power that it is destined to acquire. You see, to rid the world of non-whites, he hatched a plan to put such a potion into the world's drinking water. We have spies and allies in every country working to make this happen. It will make men look like him and women be blonde, blue-eyed, and big breasted. Everything's ready... except my potion!"

"Maybe you'll find a way."

"In the meantime, I've concocted a poison in the form of a powder that will kill all humanoid life. It's odorless, colorless, dissolves instantly when poured into liquid, and is one of the deadliest poisons known to man."

They were going to kill everyone on Earth if they couldn't get their way? "All humanoid life? Including those here? Has

Grump decided that, if whites cannot rule, then humanity should die out?"

He looked intrigued. "No. Interesting concept though. I may mention it to him. He doesn't know about the powder. It's my failsafe if I can't find a solution for my potion. It won't kill anyone here. My assistants have been placing a small but increasing dose into our water supply every day. We've been building up an immunity to the powder."

I nodded as if agreeing. "Sounds wise. I hate to trouble you, but is there any chance I might take some of it with me, to start building my own immunity? You know, in the event you aren't successful with the other potion?"

"No trouble at all! Of course. I'll have some sent to your rooms in the palace with instructions."

"Thank you."

"If you think that's something," he began, moving toward a wall of refrigerators, "look at this. I've had more success with my cure for homosexuality." He opened a fridge and pulled out a vial of rainbow-colored liquid. Somehow, the bands of color remained separated.

"How did you achieve the banding?"

He grinned. "That's a secret, but the colors are the area where all others who've tried to cure gays failed and I have succeeded. By targeting each area of gay pride, I was able to nullify the sickness. Red is for life, so blood is the obvious liquid, but it must be the blood of a heterosexual male, preferably one with a small penis. You see, the donor must have an erection at the time the blood is drained directly from the penis until it goes limp. As we all know, gays are obsessed with their large genitals, so I counteract this with a smaller source."

"Genius," I murmured, glad I could not be a donor. It sounded terribly painful. The whole idea of this potion was so ludicrous that I felt amused more than disturbed, but then it was hard to ignore the reality of the potion he'd created and consumed because it was still in effect; he looked like a white version of himself. Did this other potion actually work? Maybe it wasn't funny after all.

He continued. "Orange is for healing, and since the potion is to achieve that very result, healing a sick perversion, I went with simple orange juice. Unsweetened, of course."

"Of course. They pride themselves on how sweet they are."

He beamed. "Exactly! Now yellow is for sunlight, but we want to reverse the sunny dispositions that make gays all queer and effeminate, so I chose the moon to represent this, and as the moon is white, so must the liquid be."

"Milk?" I guessed.

"Oh no. I needed something stronger. It is sperm, from the same donor, with some yellow food coloring, of course. These machines you see on the wall, once attached to a virile man in the correct manner, can extract a healthy supply in short order. This double dose of masculinity, blood, and sperm, is crucial to the potion's success."

"Fascinating." I couldn't help looking at the devices he meant. Seeing my gaze, Karson smirked.

"I tested the machines personally. They're fabulous. I'm not allowed to use a GOP Room due to my race, so these have been a satisfying, albeit temporary replacement. Anyway, green is for nature and since homosexuality is an unnatural abomination, this part of the potion is crucial. I despaired for the right substance until it finally hit me. What is the most natural liquid in the world?"

"Water?"

"Correct!"

"But water isn't green," I observed.

"No, it isn't, but it's not blue either, and yet the ocean is that color. This is an optical illusion. Well, in a moment of supreme genius, I realized that the water will fall between the yellow and blue bands of the potion." He paused as if expecting me to figure it out. "And yellow and blue make..."

"Green."

"Yes. Simple and yet brilliant. The water is drawn from a pure spring here on the island."

"But then what did you use for blue if not water?"

"Well comrade, water would not have worked anyway for the reasons we just discussed. Blue is for harmony and peace, but there are no naturally occurring blue liquids that would suffice. However, cocktail drinks are consumed when people socialize, an act of coming together in harmony. And so, I chose blue curacao, a popular additive to cocktail drinks."

He was crazy, but I said, "You are clever beyond imagining."

"I know! The final color is purple for spirit, but it is the gay spirit that must be crushed, and so we need not something that champions the spirit, but destroys it. All alcohols, which coincidentally are called spirits, are technically depressants, which is why they put you to sleep and can make you unconscious, even cause death. And so, the final ingredient is an altered version of purple drank."

"Purple what?"

"Purple drank. It's made from cough syrup, which typically has a purple color, but this is usually combined with soda and a candy for a sweeter flavor. I instead used vodka in place of soda for an extra kick. Vodka is, of course, a spirit, but one that, if consumed in enough quantity, will suppress yours."

"Remarkable."

"I call it the 'Ben Karson.' A straight man who drinks it will never choose to be a homosexual, as they are overcome with hatred for them. Interestingly, if the banding is not maintained and the liquid is well mixed, it can turn a straight man gay, or make a gay man ever gayer. One solution to this is to do them as a series of six shots, but this seems impractical for curing gays unaware."

"How does it taste? When it's mixed?"

"Oh, it's disgusting. We had to waterboard homos to get them to drink it, so I turned this into a pill instead. It's still gross, so it's chocolate coated to help it go down easier, but you have to wait fifteen minutes for full potency. And you shouldn't go swimming for an hour."

"It sounds like some sort of miracle pill."

"Yes. If only the banding was not an issue, we could get this into the world's water supply and eradicate homosexuality in all its forms, like those big, hairy, transsexual men. As it is, it would turn the whole world gay and we can't have that. I'm still working on a way."

Well, at least one plan wasn't ready. Maybe if I killed him now, I could save the world. "As you are so resourceful, I'm sure you'll succeed."

He sighed heavily. "If only that were certain. I've had a number of failures."

"Like what?"

He took me to a doorway and pulled aside the curtain. Lying on a bed, face down, were three nude women. One was orange, one a tan color like normal Caucasian skin exposed to sun, and a third was stark white. None were moving and I sensed they hadn't in some time.

Chapter 10 – "The Golden Armory"

"I tried spray painting them," Karson began, looking at the three women, "to see if a superficial color change would make them superior to what they were born as, but their skin couldn't breathe, and they perished."

Somehow none of this surprised me. After all, it seemed that everything gold around here had merely been spray-painted that way. "What race were they?"

"Black, the darkest I could find. It would take the most to turn them."

"Of course." I felt relieved that he hadn't been able to use Jada.

He led me to another room where the smell of decaying flesh was overwhelming so that I covered my nose. A dozen bodies lay on steel tables in various stages of decomposition. All appeared to be Caucasian, though the few bodies that were partially uncovered showed significant stitching of their flesh. It almost appeared as though body parts had been sewn together. They remained me of the people I'd seen on the Safari, those scarred people who had memorized books.

"Similar experiment here," Karson began. "I skinned alive minorities and then grafted the skin of white donors onto them. Once again, this did not achieve an improvement. They were just as animalistic, if not more so, after the procedure."

"Sounds very painful."

He laughed. "Oh, it was. You should've heard the screaming, like the savages they are. We called this the Scream Emporium. If they'd had any sense of decorum, they would've born the process with grace, and looked forward to their transformation into a higher being. As it was, they acted like animals and so I let them die like animals, from gangrene. That quieted them, one by one. The others I chased away toward the Safari, the disgusting creatures."

We walked away, to my relief. "So, some of your work is about turning minorities back to their primal state, but other work is about curing or improving them. Have you given up on the latter?"

"Mostly, yes. What ails them is pathological; it can't be cured. I conducted those experiments in secret, as the emperor would not approve. He just wants anyone who is not a white, heterosexual male, or subservient female, to vanish. We all do, so that whites achieve supremacy. There should be more of us than them, of course, but the savages breed like sex-crazed rabbits. One of my ideas was to make sure that whites always have twins, so we'd populate faster and achieve dominance that way, but the emperor suggested at least triplets. I'm still working on fertility drugs to achieve this."

"Seems like a solid plan." I wandered to another freezer with a glass door, having noticed what I thought were eyeballs, rows upon rows of them. Karson joined me and opened it, a blast of frost coming out. He retrieved a tray with two eyes on it, closing the door.

"I tried injecting various compounds into their eyes to make them blue," he began, gazing at the frozen orbs.

"It worked."

"No. I mean, it did turn the eyes blue, yes, but they always went blind."

"Still attractive to look at," I said, trying to humor him.

He perked up. "Yes, there is that. Perhaps I'll do this for the concubines. What does it matter that they can't see? But for the master race, yes, we cannot all be blind."

"Yes, of course."

"I've been trying to find the gene that makes non-whites and gays inferior, but it has eluded me thus far. I know it must be there."

"Your persistence has paid off in other ways. Have you found the gene that makes women inferior?" I thought he'd approve of the question, but he gave me a withering look.

"The missing Y chromosome."

I feigned realization. "Ah, of course. It is their nature."

"Precisely."

I heard a noise to one side and turned. There stood Kahnye in a collar and white hospital gown. He clearly expected a surgery to be performed on him, and yet his tears indicated something was amiss. How much of our conversation had he heard?

"You don't mean it," he whispered, lips trembling.

Dr. Karson moved toward with genuine sympathy on his face. "Dear Kahnye, come to the table. The operation will go just as planned."

I wondered which surgery he wanted. The one to replace his skin with a white person's? To be turned into one of these monsters hunted for sport? Surely it was not to have experiments done on him for research. Or did he only wish to drink the potion Karson had thus far reserved for himself? Which doctor did he want? Dr. Frankenstein, Dr. Moreau, Dr. Josef Mengele, or Dr. Jekyll?

Kahnye backed away. Then with a strangled cry, he ran for the exit. Suddenly he let out a shriek and stopped running, grabbing at the collar furiously. I detected the faint sound of electricity humming before he fell to the ground, flopping like a fish once, twice, and then laying still. Karson turned to me with a smirk, holding up a small remote. On its white surface lay a single button with skull and crossbones painted in black.

"They sometimes forget what the collar really does." He laughed – a deep, cold sound that chilled my soul. And I took a second look at his covered neck, realizing he wore one, too. "Well my dear boy, I've enjoyed your visit, but as you can see, I have important work to attend to."

"Yes, of course. I will show myself out."

"No need," said a woman's voice behind me. Svetlana had arrived. She squeezed my ass on passing as she approached the good doctor. "The emperor would like to know if the ring is ready."

"Ah, yes. Of course. I had forgotten." He went to a cabinet and fetched a black, velvet box, bringing it to a table, where he opened it to gaze down at the contents, which I couldn't see. A look of rapture overcame his features and I thought I heard slithering voices around me, but they seemed to be coming from the box, which I moved toward. Peering inside, I saw a golden ring with fine script written all over it. A terrible longing filled my heart as fantasies of power and riches soared within me.

"My precious," Karson whispered.

At those possessive words, I felt rage overcome me and was about to club him down and leap for the ring when the box suddenly slammed shut. I blinked in surprise, feeling like ice-cold water had been splashed in my face. Having closed the box, Svetlana lifted it with a wry look at the two of us.

"Good thing it has no effect on me," she remarked, turning for the door. "Come, Max."

Still shaken by what had happened, I began to follow but then stopped for one final question. "Say," I began to Karson, "if you don't mind my asking, you seem to have a position of great responsibility. Why weren't you at the gathering of lords when I arrived?"

He smiled patiently. "That's another problem my potion will solve."

"How so?"

"Blacks aren't allowed to own land or have titles and I'm therefore unworthy until I become a white man."

"I see. Well, I wish you good luck with everything."

He nodded and I left with my handler. A short flight took us from the White Utopia Building to the Golden Armory, our next stop. The first sign that we were approaching was the rocket launch pad, replete with a missile at the ready, a giant T emblazoned on it. Several more came into view as we neared. A runway had various craft parked near it, an air traffic control tower, several large hangers, and a complex of industrial-looking buildings next to them. Ordinary planes and helicopters like the one we exited stood beside other crafts that looked like something out of a sci-fi movie. They were sleek, gold, and had wings in unusual positions or more than one pair. We approached a craft that looked like a smaller Osprey the U.C. military had, where the propellers in use as a plane could be rotated so the craft could hover.

Indicating it, Svetlana remarked, "This one, the Peregrine, is my favorite. See how it's like both a plane and helicopter? It's pressurized and can fly high and far, and yet we can land it like a helicopter. It's one-of-a-kind, but we're building a bigger one." She led me inside it, where first-class seating for a dozen awaited a lucky passenger. Everything else, from walls to tables and crystal goblets visible behind glass doors was as luxurious as expected.

We exited and headed for the nearest building, passing military guards everywhere. She explained that they were necessary due to the advanced weaponry designed, built, tested, and stored in the facility. After a maze of corridors, we stepped inside a large rectangular room with smaller ones off to each side. Everywhere I looked, men in suits or white labs coats moved about tables holding a multitude of items. Some were obviously weapons – handguns, rifles, grenade launchers, knives, crossbows and more. Others looked like jewelry while some were ordinary household items, from dishes to pens and TV remotes.

"Max," Svetlana began, leading me toward a dapper middle-aged man, who stood next to a woman, "this is Cue, our Minister of Technology."

Cue greeted us and asked for a moment to finish what he was doing. He turned back to the stunning girl, who had long blonde hair and wore silver short shorts, a matching brassiere, and boots to her knees. A few feet away were several other women, all nearly identical, though some wore lingerie. He pressed a button on a tablet and a touch of smoke puffed from one nipple of the woman's bra, while the other did nothing. He sighed.

"Still working out some kinks in the bots," he said to me. "And after all that effort to put the kink *into* them." He laughed.

I arched an eyebrow. "These are robots?"

"Femme bots, comrade. Deadly sex kittens, if that's not too redundant. These are an earlier model. You can see why I gave up on them."

"There are no fully functional ones?"

"Not of these, no. I mean they're good for sex. A man must have his priorities. But they're no good as deadly assassins. We were going to send them to other countries to seduce powerful men and then kill them after a bout of lovemaking. But I have another, newer version that works all around. The T-1000 prototype. She's remarkable. Liquid metal. Very dangerous. You'd never guess what she really is."

I looked around, my gaze sweeping over Svetlana, who winked me. "I'd love to see her."

"Can't. She's on a mission for Grump. That reminds me. Svetlana dear, would you go to lab 007? They need you in there for a bit."

"Of course. I'll return for you, Max." She turned and left.

I asked Cue, "So, what is it you do here? Svetlana was coy about that."

"Yes, she's that way about a lot of things. It's that Russian programming."

"Programming?"

He waved me off. "I make gadgets, Max. Would you care to see them?"

"Sure." I suspected that this was from where those weapons on the Safari had originated.

As he led me to a table, he remarked that he was instrumental in His Majesty's plans for world domination, for they'd either take over the world or destroy it soon enough. Aside from advanced weaponry, he made smaller items to help citizens infiltrate other countries and take control of people, places, and things.

"Take this gold watch," he said, lifting one that seemed ordinary enough. "It's packed with features. It has a Geiger counter, a laser, a grappling hook, a mine detonator, a flashlight, and a jammer."

Impressed, I asked, "A jammer?"

"Yes, it jams any signal around you if activated."

"What kind of signal? When would you use it?"

"Well, if you thought there might be a nearby listening device, for example, this transmits a signal we can't hear, but which causes silence to be the only thing that gets picked up."

I immediately wanted this and to have it activated the entire time I was in Grumpland. "What about a heart rate monitor or sleep tracking? Does the watch have those?"

He frowned at me. "Don't be stupid. The emperor couldn't care less about his health. Here, why don't you take it? This is only a prototype, but he wants it to have more diamonds anyway."

I gladly accepted the gift and put in on in a display of gratitude and acceptance of all that I saw in Grumpland. The jammer would come in handy. I then picked up a pair of spectacles. "What about these glasses?"

"X-ray vision that only works on the female form. Better to ogle them with. He doesn't need to see under men's clothing."

"Of course." I wondered how it knew the difference but didn't ask. He encouraged me to put them on. No women were allowed to work here, of course, but two slaves were cleaning in one area and they appeared nude to me. The femme bots did not, but then they weren't real people. I glanced in the direction Svetlana had gone.

Smirking at me and taking them away, Cue said, "Can't let you try that again when she comes back."

Flushing, I stammered an apology as he laughed and told me not to worry. He'd have done the same but already knew what lay under there. That startled me. To change the subject, I opened a closed jewelry box to find golden rings with flowing script written upon them, less ornate than the one back at the White Utopia Building. A similar but smaller enthrallment came over me as I counted them, wanting to try them on, but Cue closed the box.

"Nineteen," he said. "Beautiful, aren't they?"

"Yes. Why not twenty?"

"I don't know. His Majesty only asked for these nineteen. Rings of Power, he called them."

"What do they do?"

"Well, that's a bit of a secret, but these are gifts for the various leaders of the world."

"You're kidding."

"No. I was surprised myself. One is for the U.C. President, one for the Prime Minister of England, another Poohtin, the North Korean leader, the list goes on. These are to be shipped out this week. I had suggested that he have a twentieth made, one for himself, to show solidarity with the world's leaders, all of them wearing these rings but he rejected that idea and bid me speak of it no further. I'm not entirely sure what they do, but Karson would know. He did something to each of them."

"Curious," I said. A twentieth ring existed after all, destined for His Majesty, but Cue seemed unaware. I was hardly going to tell him.

"Come, let me show you something else." He led me past racks full of weaponry before stopping at a table, various items strewn about. Some looked like bombs but others ordinary items like a mug, eraser, and book. "Here we have a variety of small explosives that are disguised to look like everyday objects. I initially doubted we would have a use for them and was just amusing myself. I like to make things that explode. Call it a hobby."

Seeing him as one of the great dangers in Grumpland, I feigned approval. "As long as you don't blow yourself up, comrade. We have need of your skills."

Seeming pleased, he picked up a smartphone that was really a controller, on which he punched digital buttons. "All of these can be remotely detonated, even armed. You can just place one somewhere and no one will ever suspect until it's killing them."

I watched as he flipped through screens of pictures, each a bomb, and armed or disabled them. I had noticed that the device wasn't locked, suggesting anyone could use it if they took it, for example. "Ingenious. What's the range?"

He laughed coldly. "The planet. They're all internet connected and the batteries in the bombs can last a thousand years. We're going to ship some to various targets or have our spies leave them somewhere."

Intently curious, so I can help them be discovered, I asked, "Where do you have spies?"

He put the controller down. "Everywhere. All branches of government in many countries. There are dedicated citizens and Grump sympathizers across the Earth, from the mightiest halls of power to the remote jungles. Our empire is vast."

Just then, gunfire sounded across the room and everyone ducked. Apparently, someone had fired a gun without meaning to and Cue went over to yell at them. In the confusion, I grabbed several items, including the eraser, a lip balm, and a fidget spinner. Most importantly, I slipped the controller into my trousers and then moved elsewhere to browse other items. An assistant there asked if I wanted to see anything, so I said yes, hoping Cue didn't go back to the bomb table any time soon or realize I was the reason something was missing. I felt sweat trickle down my back. The assistant showed me a pen that was really a grappling hook; he offered it to me to keep as a souvenir, so I accepted it. He also gave me a pen drive that had a laser in it.

Without nothing else to do, I went to a window overlooking the airfield, and that's where Cue found me. To keep his mind off what I'd been up to, I asked him, "Are the launch pads outside only for missiles or do you have spacecraft as well? I thought I saw some in the hanger."

"Oh yes, but we're far ahead of everyone else. Our spacecraft can simply fly up and into space without any trouble. We've been to the moon and have a flight to Mars later this year. We only use launchpads for the missiles. We have a payload of nukes ready to deliver around the world, should the

Treasonous United Colonies try anything more than that fighter plane we shot down."

"Hail Grump. Is that the only target?"

"I'm not at liberty to say, but since you live there, you should seriously consider coming here permanently to avoid obliteration."

"Sound advice." This entire island had to be destroyed. Grump was a madman. They all were. The obvious way to do that was to get all of them to drink those vials around their necks, but that would kill the proles, who seemed more innocent, though they were all complicit. Either way, Grump had to give the order and that meant convincing him the U.C. was coming, but wouldn't they just launch these missiles if that happened? The launch mechanism would have to be destroyed first if so. I had to ask.

"Yes," replied Cue, "we would launch the missiles first and then drink. The whole world would be destroyed, as it would deserve to be."

"Where's the control room?" I asked. "Might I see how it works?"

He smiled. "I can show it to you, but how it works is highly classified."

"Of course."

I followed him down a few halls and into a bunker, where several men were stationed at computers, a large screen on the wall showing flight traffic across the Atlantic Ocean. This was presumably how they'd known about the U.C. fighter jet they'd shot down. Cue confirmed this when asked, then showed me which computers did what, and finally the one for the missile launches. While he was talking, I had one hand in a pocket, fingering the fidget spinner and the eraser. After a moment, I feigned a sneeze, pulled my hand out of my pocket with the fidget spinner palmed out of sight, and grabbed a tissue, discreetly dropping the spinner into the tissue box as Cue kept talking. I wiped my nose with that tissue and a second, then looked around for a trash bin. On seeing one, I dropped the tissues and the eraser into it. Maybe I'd get a chance to blow this up, but I doubted it.

Moments later, Svetlana rejoined us and suggested we had better get going. I said my farewells to Cue, hoping to escape here without him realizing anything. As a bit of subterfuge, I asked what his plans were as if I was hoping he'd join me for dinner, but he was headed to a GOP Room, to which I suggested he get going before all the best girls were taken. He perked up and thanked me for the idea, and on leaving, he went in a direction different from the room where we'd met. With any luck, he wouldn't return tonight.

Having pilfered what I could, with my mind on some sort of plan forming, I followed Svetlana back to the golden limo. She tried to seduce me along the way, joking that I wouldn't want Ebony Girl anymore after a tryst with her, but I demurred, and she teased me that I was in love. I used that as a chance to remind her that I had wanted Ebony Girl to come to my rooms again this night, and for her to arrange a visit from the boy, David. I suggested both be brought to me for dinner in my rooms and while Svetlana expressed some frustration with the idea, claiming I was being too nice to a slave and the boy shouldn't be pampered either, she relented, admitting that Grump was elsewhere that night anyway.

When we arrived at the palace, she dropped me off and left to retrieve them. Relieved for a chance to be alone, I quickly reached my suite and hid the gadgets. I only needed to remain undiscovered until the morning when Hillary Fest began, and I attempted something I likely shouldn't. I now feared that if I remained the full two weeks, I'd be corrupted beyond repair. And what I'd learned today added urgency to warning those in power back in the U.C. about what he was planning, as multiple plots were imminent. They might not believe me alone, however. With both Jada and David along, they might, and Hillary would certainly be taken seriously. And she had the ability to fly us out of here. A rough plan solidified a little more as I prepared for the night, ordering dinner from a servant and taking a shower.

As I sat sipping wine from the ever-present decanters of it, a knock on the door sounded. On opening it, I saw a frightened David standing beside a stern woman who I took to be one of the school's staff. By her attire, which was a clean, neat, and form-fitting dress with cleavage from neck to belly, I knew her to be in the Outer Party. By contrast, poor David was a prole and dressed the part, in dirty, faded, and worn grey shorts and shirt, socks, and shoes. He looked cold.

The woman bowed, called me "My lord," and said she'd brought "the boy" as directed. I thanked and excused her, but she started to give David some warnings about how he was to behave until I told her I would handle it and closed the door in her face. I suspected she was part of the problem.

"Don't you have a jacket?" I asked him.

David shook his head. He seemed muted. Had he closed back up since I'd seen him last?

"Are you cold?" I asked.

From the way he looked up at me, I knew the answer was yes but that he'd likely been taught not to complain and wasn't going to admit it. He shook his head, but I brought him over to the fireplace. He stared into the crackling flames, mesmerized, and as I watched him, I made a decision and called for a servant, ordering him fresh clothing. I then took him to the bathroom for a hot bath, which he didn't seem to know how to do for himself, so I had to wash the grime from his frail body. By the time he stood wrapped in plush towel, which I noticed him snuggling against, the change of clothes had arrived, and I dressed him. By now he'd relaxed and even smiled, revealing poor dental hygiene. Spare toothbrushes were handy and so I soon had him taken care of, even clipping his overgrown nails, which he'd been biting or tearing off. The neglect resonated from him.

We went to the couch, where I slowly got him to tell me about his life. He didn't know who his parents were. Whether he had brothers or sisters was unknown. I wondered if I could find out, as this could give him comfort. I asked what he did after school, but he said lessons were taught throughout the day, with short breaks from time to time. During these, he and the others were required to watch Grump TV, undoubtedly for propaganda films. I asked about books only to have him repeat the idea that books are evil and should be reported to teachers immediately so they could be burned.

He finally worked up the courage to ask me about myself, and when I said I had been born and raised in the United Colonies and still lived there, he let out a small cry of fear and recoiled, pulling away on the couch with his knees up under his chin. It took ten minutes to calm him, and though I was ashamed of my role in the Golden Cruises, I had to tell him about that, and that I was a Republican and not a Democrat, to ease his fears. He perked up when he learned that I was "that man" in the Treasonous United Colonies sending people here. I ruefully admitted it again before telling him life in Amnesia wasn't bad like he'd been taught, but he didn't believe me. Nothing would change his mind unless he saw it with his own eyes.

Another knock on the door preceded Jada stepping in and closing it behind her. I'd instructed servants to get her some functional clothes that were superior to her normal, worn attire, and they'd complied. She wore it now, fur-lined suede trousers and matching sweater that were otherwise simple but attractive on her. She joined David and I as I made introductions, but this didn't go well. Just as he'd been taught about how evil Amnesians were, he believed teachings about blacks being inferiors who deserved to be slaves. Maybe this was a mistake, having them both here. A lifetime of racism might hinder my plans. If these two couldn't get along, rescuing both of them would be harder. I needed him to follow her directions when I wasn't around tomorrow and not to cause a fuss that would get both of them in trouble, or make them harder to rescue.

Fortunately, he'd been taught to respect members of the Inner and Outer party, and while I technically was neither, he feared my disapproval and kept negative comments about Jada to himself. The look of disapproval didn't disappear from his eyes, even when food arrived and he hungrily eyed it. We moved to the table, with me at the head and my guests facing each other on either side.

"Slaves aren't allowed at the table," he quietly observed, as if fearful what I'd say.

"She's my guest."

"He's right, though. Better not let anyone else see this." She smiled at David. "Are you going to keep my secret?"

He frowned at her, but then nodded.

I took a pastry and handed it to him, wondering if rewarding him might help. "I knew you were a good boy."

As we began to eat, I tried to get them talking to each other. At first, he refused to say much, as if she was beneath him. I realized he'd been taught not to ask questions, but natural curiosity took over when we started answering him. What he asked me showed just how uneducated he really was. Jada answered him as often as I did, and he soon hung on our every word as we told him things he'd wanted to know. Once we'd hooked him, all traces of holding back disappeared. We showed him a respect he'd likely never known, and he became enthusiastic, seeming to forget how he was supposed to view Jada.

"Is it true that you don't get to come to the afterlife with us?" David asked her, fingering the vial around his neck, eyes on her bare nape, where her vial would've been but wasn't.

"Yes."

"But I want you to come with us."

Jada smiled. "That's sweet. But I'd rather you stay here with me."

He looked away. "But I don't like it here." He seemed to mean being on Earth. His eyes warily turned to me as if he was afraid that he'd admitted something he shouldn't.

I said, "It's okay, David. I don't like it here either."

"You don't?" He scanned the luxury around us.

"Well," I began, clarifying, "these riches are nice, but they don't belong to me. I don't have this at home, but what I have is still good, and enough for me. I don't like what I see here in Grumpland for people like yourself, how you have to live."

"Then why do you tell people to come here on the Golden Cruises?"

"Great question. I didn't realize things weren't going well for people here, but now I do."

"Does that mean you won't send people here anymore?"

"Maybe. I haven't decided. But I think the important part for me is that I'm leaving soon, maybe as soon as tomorrow."

"Can I come with you?" he interrupted, face full of hope. As it turns out, that's exactly where I was headed.

"I'm hoping so, but it's a secret, okay? Do you know how to keep a secret?"

He nodded vigorously.

"What's a secret you aren't supposed to tell?" Jada asked.

He opened his mouth to say it, then realized her ploy and smiled. "You tried to trick me!"

We all laughed.

We continued eating, David asking a torrent of questions. Many were directed at Jada, as he learned how poorly the slaves live and couldn't believe what he was hearing.

"Can she come with us?" he asked me.

"That's my hope," I replied. "What I'd like is for you two to remain here in my rooms tomorrow, and when ready, I'm hoping to come get both of you and we'll all leave together. How's that sound?"

"Great!"

Jada looked at me quizzically but seemed to understand that I wasn't going to give details now. As David ate his fill, he began to yawn more and more, so we left the table. He sat on the couch next to Jada, who put an around him, and before long he'd decided to lie down with his head on her lap. He drifted off to sleep and Jada soon extricated herself so we could talk without disturbing him, a blanket laid across the sleeping boy.

"Is this plan of yours dangerous?" she asked, looking dubious.

"For me, yes. I don't think it will be for you two, as you'll be here. If I never show up again, you'll know I failed, but you can just say I asked you to stay here. Both of you. No one needs to know anything else."

"What are you planning to do?"

"I need to rescue Hillary from the wicker statue. I need her help to get you out of here because I don't know how to fly the craft I have in mind and she likely does. I don't want to tell you too much more."

"It's okay. I trust you."

She wrapped her arms around me, and we stayed up for a few hours, drinking wine and talking, before going to bed, where I found it hard to sleep. I'd get a far better sense of how likely my plan was on seeing the Wicker Statue, but until then, I could only wonder what I'd find. I hadn't really done anything wrong yet other than pilfer a few bombs and the controller, but as the former were all ordinary items, it was likely no one would know I had them. If I couldn't pull this off, I'd just ditch them and the controller somewhere, each separate, after wiping my fingerprints from them. Abandoning the plan posed no risk, as I'd committed to nothing yet.

I stayed up long into the night, the fireplace crackling across the room, my eyes moving from it to my guests, and to the dark window and the hulking Mt. Grumpmore out in the cold night. Orange lights shown on it so that even in darkness, there was no escape from the sneering, contemptuous gaze of Grump. With the gusts of wind tearing at the slopes, the lights jiggled and moved, making it appear as though flames danced wickedly across Grump's features, a macabre scene. Light shone in the eyes of all five heads, suggesting he kept watch over everyone here, just as I kept watch over my charges this night.

Suddenly I went cold on remembering that my room was likely bugged or had cameras recording everything. What I fool I was! I'd become so wrapped up in trying to ease David's fears that I had forgotten to activate the jammer in my watch. My heart pounded as I listened for the heavy footsteps coming toward my door, to break it down, storm the room, and arrest all three of us. I stood frozen for long moments, hearing nothing but the sound of my own heavy breathing. Did they know? Were they waiting? Or were they getting ready and just hadn't gotten here yet? Was Grump going to pretend everything was alright only to surprise me at the last moment? It seemed the kind of torture he'd enact

Feeling my legs tremble, I sat on the couch and put my head in my heads, images of my execution flashing in my head. I'd likely be burned alive along with Hillary as a traitor from the Treasonous United Colonies. My eyes darted to the cabinet where I'd hidden my gadgets. I should've taken something with real firepower, but all of the weapons had been too large and conspicuous. There was no hope for it anyway. If they knew, I'd never get out of here, and certainly not with Jada and David. I'd been coy about my plans to them, creating plausible deniability that they'd had any idea what I was up to, but that might've been ruined so utterly that I almost wanted to laugh.

Then I stopped short. Hadn't I set the jammer to be on all the time? I checked the display and saw the little x over the ear icon. It had been on the whole time anyway. I laughed and wanted to cry at the same time. I was losing my mind. This place was getting to me. I had to get out of here. Trying to make myself relax, I paced before the fireplace, sometimes stopping to tuck in David more or put a comforting hand on him as he stirred from some unknown nightmare. I'd seen enough of the island now and all the pieces came together in my head. I finally forced myself into bed beside Jada so that I'd be rested for a big day ahead, one that, in all likelihood, would end with me dead.

Chapter 11 – "Hillary Fest"

In the morning, I woke to find Jada on one side and David on my other, curled up beside me and snoring. The guards hadn't stormed the room. I lay there for a while, letting them sleep, knowing that Hillary Fest was the only event today and I, therefore, had a quiet morning before Svetlana collected me for either that or my execution. Danger loomed, and regardless of what was to come, these were the final peaceful moments of my day, possibly my life, and I was loath to get up and face reality.

Before long, both Jada and David had woken, and we had a quiet breakfast delivered to my rooms. I dismissed a passing thought that the food might be poisoned because that was far too private a way for me to be killed. Was the room not bugged after all? Was it bugged but no one had been paying attention? Had my status made them lax in their security measures? I tried to not look worried, especially for David's sake, but Jada's repeated looks of concern at me made me realize I wasn't hiding it well. I had to do better when I left here so that Svetlana, who had a keen eye, suspected nothing. I practiced with my guests, while Jada and I tried to find ways to make David laugh and act like a child with nothing to worry about. He frequently hugged us both and asked if he could stay forever, and this is when I told him part of my plan.

"You'll both wait here for me to return. I want you to focus on remaining quiet. I will tell the maids to leave my rooms untouched."

"They will obey because of who you are," she observed.

Choosing my words carefully in case anyone was listening now, I said, "Let's hope so. When I get back, I'll see if both of you will be able to come with me as I leave Grumpland."

David asked without fear, "Are we going to Amnesia?"

I noticed he seemed curious, not frightened, but I still didn't want to tell him yes. "We'll go somewhere safe, okay? All three of us together."

He smiled and nodded, reaching for another bite. I pulled Jada aside and whispered to her about my fears that if I tried and failed before reaching them, that they might be suspected of being part of the plot anyway. She had to convincingly tell Grump that I had commanded them to remain until I returned that night. Whatever he told them about my behavior at Hillary Fest, she had to act shocked, which was one reason I wasn't telling her the plan. The other reason was that I wasn't sure what, if anything, I was going to do, not to mention how.

She understood and said she would keep them safe and quiet for the day while awaiting my return. I kissed her once more, then got myself ready, putting all of the gadgets I needed into appropriate hiding places on myself. Then I left my rooms, finding a servant to give instructions to, and went to the palace lobby.

Along the way, neither guards nor Inner Party members seemed at all concerned about me. I scrutinized each while trying to pretend I wasn't doing so, looking for any subtle signs that I was suspected. I put on my own show of normalcy and felt more at ease as time passed without anyone acting strangely toward me. On arrival, Svetlana greeted me in her usual way, with a flirtatious look and some minor groping. Fortunately, I hadn't hidden anything in a pocket near my ass.

"You seem a little tense," she remarked, squeezing my butt a second time. I forced myself to relax my muscles and shrugged.

"Just excited about today, comrade, and what we're going to see. Curiosity has gotten the better of me."

She hooked her arm with mine and led me to the golden limo. "The spectacle is always special. You won't be required to make a speech or anything, so you should just enjoy the show."

"Yes, but I was hoping to speak with Crooked Hillary one last time. I suspect she'll be up in the wicker statue and the heights might make me queasy."

She believed this lie. "I didn't realize you were such a softy. You handled the Safari so well."

"Everyone has their fear."

"Not me."

We drove a short way to where Hillary Fest was to happen on the other side of the rolling hills that blocked the view of the Wicker Hillary from town. A line of cars that held Inner and Outer Party members let us speed by, as our golden limo indicated our superiority. Proles had to hoof it and always cheered us from their positions along the roadside as we passed. When we crested a hill, I saw a statue, a hundred feet tall, soaring into the azure sky but covered by a golden sheet with a giant T on it. A low platform and stage surrounded it. A huge throng of worshippers stood quietly before it, guards keeping them in line. Somewhere up there, likely under that sheet, the real Hillary awaited her death.

"Now's probably a good time," I began, "to talk with the prisoner, to get her final thoughts before execution. The emperor might enjoy knowing how terrified she is, and he can use what I learn to humiliate her long after he's killed her."

Svetlana beamed at me. "Wonderful idea, Max. We may have just enough time to get you up there and back down again. Come."

The driver parked and we left the car, which had gone around to the secured area behind the stage and statue. I saw Hunter One and all of its weapons there. It gave me an idea. Several other military vehicles were near but were mostly personnel carriers. A host of armed men stood idly about. Another golden limo, presumably the one for Grump, sat nearby. A line of porta potties was beside a command tent and a large storage shed, which gave the impression of being the place where the Wicker Hillary was constructed.

We made our way up to the platform, then behind the golden sheet so that we stood inside both the covering and the statue that loomed high above us. Several inches of space separated each piece of wicker so that one could see through much of the structure. At the statue's front, I saw dozens of the bibliophiles Grump had captured on the S, each one lashed to the wicker support beams and ready to be burned alive for their love of books. Granger, Millie, the little girl, all of them were here, stripped naked. I could see the bruises and cuts from having been beaten and whipped, their stitched-together skin even more tortured. I had forgotten they'd be here and wondered if there was some way to free them, too.

Svetlana gestured to the spiral staircase built into the interior of the wicker statue and I began to ascend. Seeing her ready to follow, I remarked that I was sure I could find my way without her. She patted my butt and let me go up alone. The climb was arduous, my legs burning by the time I reached the back of the statue's neck, where a locked door barred the way. A crude wooden key hung nearby but far enough to prevent the prisoner from reaching it. I used it to unlock the door and entered, finding a final stairway leading up to the head, where Hillary sat watching me approach, her blank expression unreadable.

Alert, intelligent brown eyes appraised me frankly. She was tall and lean, her muscled physique easy to see because she still wore the lingerie Grump has presumably put her in. Aside from the hair color, she didn't resemble Crooked Hillary at all, though from a distance, no one would know. I doubted they cared. For a woman facing her execution, she seemed quite stoic. It would be no ordinary demise. A chant of "burn her" began far below. We gazed silently at each other before I finally spoke.

"I don't have much time."

"Neither do I." Her voice was stronger than I expected.

"I'm here to rescue you."

She snorted. "I don't see that happening."

"I can get you out of here. I need you to get me, yourself, and a few others out of here, off this island."

Unimpressed, she remarked, "I know who you are, Max. I've seen your broadcasts and know you're in league with him."

I shook my head. "Not anymore. I didn't realize how awful this place would be."

"You should've."

"I know. I heard what Grump haters said about him and thought they were wrong, but I know better. You've seen some of what I mean."

"More than you think."

I changed tactics. "You have nothing to lose by trying to escape. It's me that does by helping you."

She considered that a moment. “Fair enough. Who are these people you want to rescue?”

“A boy and a woman.”

“So, chivalry isn’t dead?”

“Look, we don’t have time for banter.” I pulled a pen from one pocket and extended it toward her. “It’s a grappling hook. You should be able to reach the ground with it. It’ll be faster than the stairs.”

She took it. “And then what? Unless you’re gonna fly us off this island, it’s pointless.”

I nodded. “There’s a craft we can use. I’m not sure of its range, but it’s at the Golden Armory. I can get us there.”

“Do you know how to fly it?”

“I was hoping you’d figure it out.”

She nodded halfheartedly. “There’s no guarantee either of us can get out of here. Why don’t you just tell me where the lab is, and I’ll go it alone?”

I shook my head. “They’ll know how you got out of here.”

Hillary pursed her lips. “Yeah, okay. Are you sure you want to do this? You’re risking your life for me.”

“Yes. I have others I need to help. I can’t save everyone, but at least those two.” Suddenly I heard someone climbing the stairs. “Wait until they light the fire. Try to play your role that you’re terrified. I’ll leave the door unlocked and you can make it down the back. I’ll be waiting with a car.”

I had to stop then, for a menacing looking Zarof had reached the door. “Out!” he barked. I cast a final look at Hillary before obeying. I tried to get the hunt master to go down before me so I could leave the cell unlocked, but he took the key, locked it, and then threw down to the base. "Won't be needing that anymore."

Frustrated, I descended with him close behind, reaching the bottom. Zarof motioned me to get away, but I asked, "Can I talk with the other sacrifices for a moment?"

He sighed impatiently. "Two minutes. Then out." He stomped away. I looked up. I'd never make it to the top in time. Hillary would have to find some way to escape the cell without my help. I had to get ready and yet be prepared to do nothing if she never made it out of there, in which case no one would know I'd done anything. Except I was about to risk it all for someone else, doubting my own intelligence as I started to do so.

Hidden from view by the giant sheet surrounding the statue, I hurriedly approached the nearest captive, who happened to be their leader, Granger. From my pocket, I pulled out the laser thumb drive I'd stolen from the Golden Lab, wishing I'd given it to Hillary. I cut through the bonds on his hands and handed the device to him, explaining that when I left, he should do the same to his feet and then free everyone else.

"But how are we to escape?" he asked.

"Just free everyone else and then resume your positions as if you're still bound. They'll drop the curtain. When they light the fire, run. There are cars behind here. You should be able to get to one, with some help from me."

"What then? We'll never make it."

"Try to reach the districts. There are people there who can take you in and hide you. Tell them Jada sent you and ask for the Underground Railroad. And if you don't make it, better to die fighting than like this."

He nodded, face grim. "Thank you."

I shook his offered hand and then walked outside the statue and its covering, finding Zarof and Svetlana making out. I cleared my throat, but they didn't separate, so I glanced around and made note of how many guards were around, what the car drivers were doing, and generally scoped out the likelihood of any of us escaping this compound alive.

I first went to a porta-potty and used it, then exited holding my stomach as if it was still upset. I approached the driver of my vehicle and inquired as to whether any medicine was inside. He said yes and opened the trunk, revealing a bag that he let me root through while he stepped away. I pretended to take something, closed the trunk, and then stood by him, chatting idly about his life as a member of the Outer Party and one of Grump's drivers, as if this was part of my reporting. He was happy to oblige. This was all done to lower his guard. I parted ways with him and approached a group of soldiers, repeating the same ruse and making myself seem like just another person hanging around this area. All the while, I kept an eye on the lone man beside Hunter One. Meanwhile, out front, Grump began his speech.

"You know we've been doing this for a long time now," he was now saying. "A long time. But today will be the best one ever. Everyone says so. Everyone. Because she's going to go through some things. Today we're going to burn Hillary for real!"

As the crowd roared, the giant sheet over the Wicker Hillary partially fell away, one corner snagged on her head and ruined the drama of it. After a moment, I heard a shot ring out and saw a man near the platform fly backward as an explosion of red flew out of his head. The drivers beside me laughed, and on seeing my confusion, one of them said the dead man had been responsible for the reveal gone wrong. Someone had just killed him, likely on Grump's order. Another shot rang out and a piece of wicker flew into the air from where the cloth was snagged. Now the cloth fell to the ground as a cheer rose from the crowd. One of the men remarked how good a shot Zarof was and I realized he'd shot away whatever the cloth had been snagged on. The huntmaster was likely to be a problem. I started for Hunter One, my eyes glancing up toward Hillary. Was she finding some way out of the cell?

Grump asked the crowd, "Did everyone watch me hunt Barak on the Safari?" They cheered at the rhetorical question, as everyone was required to do so. "He was an animal. And he was a gutless animal. He was crying, and screaming, and whimpering. He was scared out of his mind. He died like a dog. He died like a coward. He was vicious and violent. He spent his last moments in a total panic, and dread, terrified of the great Donald Grump, your emperor."

The crowd roared.

The guard beside Hunter One recognized me and said around a cigarette, "Hey Max. You aren't up there watching the show?"

"No. I can hear it from here. His Majesty wanted me to get a good look at Hunter One here. Do you mind showing me how these gadgets work?"

"Anything for the emperor," he replied, tossing the cancer stick aside. He motioned for me to get in behind the driver's seat, telling me how the vehicle started and that it had an autopilot that would return it to various locations, which included the palace. I humored him about these features and feigned interest even though the weapons were my main concern. I was about to have need of them.

Grump's voice rang out again. "You know what else we found on the Safari? Book lovers!"

The crowd booed.

"Yeah, I hate books, too," he continued, "except for the ones I've written. Those are great, aren't they?"

Everyone cheered.

"But these book lovers we found weren't reading my books. Do you know what they were doing? It's really terrible. Just terrible. They had memorized forbidden books, and they were pacing around like madmen, reciting them to themselves over and over. Just pathetic."

The crowd jeered.

To laughter, he then moaned gibberish as if that was how Granger and the others had been acting at the time. "Does everyone remember what we do with books?"

"Burn them! Burn them! Burn them!"

Grump let this chant go on for several minutes, during which the guard showed me how to use several of the weapons. Most were largely foolproof. You just turned them on, aimed, and fired. Some hardly needed aiming because they shot something with a wide arc and which killed everything in its path. A few took a minute to charge, but once ready, they were good for quite a few shots until the battery died down. When I asked how they prevented the wrong people from using this, he laughed and said only the proles were considered such people and they'd never get anywhere near them. There weren't any safeguards at all.

"Today's a kind of two for one deal," said Grump. "We're not only burning these hideous creatures you see here at the bottom of Wicker Hillary, but the captured pilot Hillary, from the Treasonous United Colonies!"

"Hail Grump!"

"Are you ready?" he asked.

In response, the crowd chanted, "Burn her!" once more. I glanced upward and thought I saw Hillary kicking at the wicker, timing her blows to the chant so that no one would hear. Had she broken through yet? There was no point in sacrificing myself if she hadn't.

"Are you ready?" Grump repeated, and the crowd grew louder. Even the guards and drivers near me began chanting. I joined in and looked up one more time. I saw Hillary's foot kick through a piece of wicker that leaned out sharply but didn't fall. She looked to be wrestling with it now, to get it aside and make room for her. I flicked a button on the plasma gun, hearing the familiar whine as it started charging, but the guard didn't seem to notice, caught up as he was in chanting. He jumped down from the vehicle to the ground.

"Light her up!" yelled Grump.

And the chanting turned to a roar as flames ignited all around the front and sides of Wicker Hillary, but not the back. At the same moment, the bibliophiles ran from the fire toward me and down the stairs. I realized they'd need cover to escape. I hesitated about revealing myself, but then I saw Hillary hanging from the rear of the statue, beginning a quick slide to the ground. Unsure what was happening, some in the crowd continued to cheer while others booed or raised shouts of alarm.

"Sorry about this," I said to the guard.

He turned toward me inquisitively and I fired. In an instant, he was gone, vaporized. I turned the weapon toward other guards and drivers, none of whom had noticed my action. I fired again and they were gone. A few other lone guards were nearby and saw this, but realizing that they were vastly outgunned, they fled. Then I heard gunshots and saw a running bibliophile clutch at his back, falling to the ground. Another shot and another one fell. Someone, likely Zarof, was picking them off from behind. I began yelling at them and motioning them out of my line of fire, but they didn't seem to understand until I aimed above their heads and pulled the trigger. A beam tore through a few guards and others there. Hillary began sprinting toward me, catching up with the bibliophiles and making them head for other vehicles. They began to get into them and drive away as I laid down cover fire.

Hillary ran up to me, looking fierce and excited as she leapt into Hunter One. "Drive!" she yelled, taking over for me at the plasma gun. I didn't have to ask if she believed me now.

Heart pounding, I leapt into the front seat and started the car. At that moment, Zarof and Svetlana appeared atop the stairs, which they ran down toward us. Hillary aimed at them and fired as my heart sank that the lovely Svetlana would be no more. As expected, the beam vaporized the hunt master. But not Svetlana, whose skin disappeared to reveal a liquid metal body that continued running toward us. Hillary let out a cry of astonishment.

"A femme bot!" I said in realization. "She's the working femme bot Cue told me about!"

"How do I kill it?"

I stomped on the gas and turned the vehicle away. "Try something else!"

Hillary moved to a more traditional weapon and trained it on the T-1000, firing. The bullets seemed to go right through it, taking pieces of liquid metal with them. The cyborg kept running as Hillary moved to the grenade launcher, the explosions buffeting Svetlana but not stopping her, though a direct hit did make her pause as her body had been contorted into a lopsided mess that couldn't run. We watched in horror as she reformed herself and resumed running. By now we were entering the road, the bibliophiles far ahead of us in multiple vehicles. The Wicker Hillary was now engulfed in flames,

"Try the heat cannon!" I yelled.

"Which one is that?"

"Behind me."

Hillary moved to it and turned it on, cursing as it warmed up and the T-1000 steadily gained. Hunter One wasn't designed for speed and we'd be in trouble if one of these weapons didn't destroy the cyborg. The cannon finally beeped that it was ready, and Hillary aimed and fired. The same circle of red light that had disintegrated Barry flew across the earth and passed over Svetlana, setting on fire the vegetation it passed over. Seeing this, the T-1000 tried to leap over it, but the circle was apparently tracking her and shifted, catching her in midair. With a poof, the liquid metal vaporized in a puff of white smoke. Svetlana was gone.

Hillary let out a shout and yelled, "You're terminated, bitch!"

"Stay back there in case there's trouble."

We continued in relative peace down the highway, eyes on the sky, roads, and wilderness. Danger could come from anywhere. When we reached the turnoff toward the districts, the cars carrying the bibliophiles peeled off with a honking of horns. Hopefully, they'd find shelter and ditch those cars somewhere. Hillary and I continued.

"How far is it?" she asked.

"A few minutes. We need to pass the palace and get through town on the way to the Golden Lab."

"Something tells me that's going to be a problem."

I hoped she was wrong. "Stay alert."

As we neared the palace, a car sometimes passed the other way, but they were never of the military type and seemed unconcerned. No one knew our destination, but they had to know there were limited ways off the island. I doubted anyone would suspect we were ultimately headed for the Peregrine, that plane and helicopter hybrid Svetlana had shown me. But first, I had to stop at the palace and get David and Jada. To reach the Peregrine, we'd need to pass it anyway. We hadn't seen any sign that anyone knew of what we'd done. Was this limited traffic normal? Had the road been cleared? What trouble lay ahead?

We approached the palace exit. Farther down the road, where we'd need to go next, multiple vehicles blocked the way. None seemed as formidable as ours until a shaft of blue light flew toward us, dissipating before reaching us. I swore and turned toward the building. By the time we got Jada and David, more such vehicles would be here, and we'd never get away. I drove right up the palace steps before crashing into the glass doors just enough to make them shatter so we could get in without trouble. No one seemed to be there as we entered the building and ran.

Chapter 12 – "A Stairway to Heaven"

We hadn't gone far in our sprint through the palace when we rounded a corner and came face to face with Grump Jr., Eric, and Jaryd. The latter hissed like a cat on seeing Hillary. Eric made a face like he'd stepped in something. Then there was Donald's oldest son.

Snootily, Jr. said, "Ugh, a whore and a traitor!"

"Well if it isn't the three little bitchkateers," Hillary mocked, eyes flashing. "Run home to your mommies before you get hurt."

Jr. straightened his jacket and tie before making a fist with his thumb inside it. "I will apprehend these two. Stand back!" He confidently approached Hillary and wound back his arm. "I will teach you a less..."

She clubbed his jaw so hard that the sound of it shattering could clearly be heard. He fell lifeless to the floor, sightless eyes gazing upward. Somehow, in death, they seemed no more vacant than a moment earlier. On seeing this, Eric backed up so hastily that he tripped, fell backward, and cracked his head on the tiles, where a pool of blood began to form from his limp body. Hillary turned toward Jaryd, who screamed like a girl and turned into a bat that flew through the nearest window. I ran to the window, wondering if we could quickly find a weapon that could shoot him from the sky, but suddenly there was no need. Jaryd flew from the shade into the sunlight and burst into flames. The writhing creature fell to the ground, a trail of smoke rising into the sky.

Hillary shook her head. "This place is far too strange."

"At least the world is rid of three of them."

"We still have to get rid of the worst one."

"Amen. Let's go. First, we need to get to my rooms, then find somewhere to hide and make a plan for how to reach the Peregrine."

She followed me as we ran along corridors I knew fewer people would be in. It became clear that word had spread and we were fugitives, for several Inner Party members called me a traitor after I'd already run by them, the cowards. Fortunately, everyone got out of the way except for a few slaves, who sometimes discreetly gestured toward one hall or another.

"They're helping us," I observed, out of breath.

"No shit."

We rounded a corner to find a sinister, roiling black cloud forming in the air ahead of us. It grew to the size of a small man. Out stepped the Grim Reaper, scythe in hand, flaming but still beady eyes on us. A skeletal hand pointed us as McKonnell leered in anticipation. Showing speed I wouldn't have imagined, he glided forward, the peculiar locomotion all the more hideous for its unnaturalness.

"What is that?" Hillary asked.

"Death!"

"Literally?"

"Yes. Run!"

We sprinted away, Mitch's hollow laughter chasing us onward. From hall to hall we fled, often passing through rooms, losing ground with every step, until finally, we neared a guarded door. Two men pointed rifles at us only to stare in horror at the Grim Reaper looming behind us. They ran, so we sprinted for the door, bashing it open to find ourselves in Grump's treasure room. Amidst the tables and assorted machinery for counting lay bag after bag of money. As I started for the exit on the far side, Hillary stopped.

"Wait! I have an idea!" She reached into a bag of money, grabbed a handful of bills, and hurled them toward Mitch. But the Grim Reaper hardly glanced at the riches.

"Not enough!" I shouted, realizing her intent. I threw two more handfuls, and this time the Grim Reaper at least appraised the bills as they fell before him. But he didn't slow. I grabbed the bag and began to run, Hillary doing the same with another. We began dumping the money as we went, and though our pace slowed, so too had McKonnell's. He finally stopped, tortured eyes darting between us and the fortune. Seeing my chance, I took both my bag and Hillary's and ran toward an open window. Behind me, I heard an agonized howl of "Nooooooooo!!!"

With a heave, I hurled the twin bags of booty through the window and they plummeted toward the marbled paving below. A high-pitched shriek rang out behind me. A black shape buffeted me aside before flying out the window after it.

"There's no telling how long that will last," I said, turning away in relief.

"Until he gets a better offer."

"No doubt. Let's go. I think we had better hide and think of a plan."

"Where? The whole island is looking for us."

My mind raced until I remembered a room, I'd barely glimpsed days before on my tour with Svetlana. I wanted to go get David and Jada, but for now, they were safer where they were. They weren't implicated in what I was doing now but the moment they were seen with me again, they would be. Taking her by the hand, I crept toward Ivanaka's rooms and stole inside. No one was there. Hillary kept watch as I moved to the statue of a nude boy. I yanked once on the penis and watched as the secret chamber swung upon. I ushered Hillary inside. We closed the door and moved farther inward and around a corner. It was dark but we feared to turn on a light until I remembered the gold watch I wore. I tapped its screen and a soft glow surrounded us. A few more taps and it turned into a kind of wide-beam flashlight.

"We should be safe here," I remarked.

"Hopefully. What is this place?"

"Some hidden room of Ivanaka's. They're so deplorable and open about it that I can't help wondering what horrors are actually hidden here. Maybe we should have a look around."

She didn't respond. Since she was still wearing lingerie, she rooted through a pile of spare clothes and found something suitable, though it wasn't quite the right fit, the style gaudy. She tore off the more offensive parts of it and donned a pair of shoes, saying they were close enough.

Then I found myself starting to tell her about all the plots I'd learned about. Karson's poison to kill everyone. The nuclear missiles. The melting ice cap. All of it. The number of plans ready, or nearly so, made an impression on Hillary, who said we had to find a way to destroy all of them, but nothing could do that. Any attack on Grumpland would bring about the end of the world, or Grumpageddon, as she called it.

"After all the time waited to be burned alive," she started, "I just want to see my wife one last time."

"You're a lesbian?" I asked in surprise. She nodded and I remarked with a grin, "Grump's Trifecta of Evil."

She arched an eyebrow. "The what? Oh, Jesus. Let me guess. Non-white, non-male, and non-hetero?" When I nodded, she added, "If we get the chance, Grump's mine. I get to kill him personally."

"Fair enough."

She tapped my shoulder and pointed. There, in the corner and hanging on the wall, was a giant velvet curtain that appeared to be hiding something behind it. We moved toward it, and as I trained the light upon it, Hillary pulled aside the curtain and I gasped.

A portrait more than ten feet tall hung in a gilded frame. It showed a figure reclining on an ornate throne, both legs spread and one draped over the chair's arm. Thin, grey hair hung from a mostly balding head with mottled flesh, a tilted, dainty crown comically standing above it all. Large bags hung beneath cold, bloodshot, sunken eyes. A crooked, broken nose had green snot pouring from it over cracked, ruby lips, behind which was a gaping maw, crooked and chipped teeth, and a forked, black tongue. Hollow cheeks wore a pink rouge that was part of a makeup application seemingly meant to bring forth beauty, but which only made the cruel, sneering, haughty expression all the more hideous and clownlike.

Jowls split the multiple chins of a thick neck, around which hung a diamond necklace. Blood, wine, and bodily fluids stained what little finery the beast wore, the brocaded lace and silk mottled. The two sagging, lumpy breasts that rested on rolls of belly fat were not the only indication of gender, for the spread legs offered a grisly view of a hairy, crab-infected vagina with puss-oozing sores. Broken and pudgy fingers with missing, split, or garishly painted nails were adorned with two and three golden rings apiece, but one stood above the others for its royal seal – the only potential indication of who this portrait immortalized. But I had never seen a member of the Grump royal family who looked like this. Or at least, not on the outside. They probably all looked like this on the inside.

Suddenly we heard a gasp. We turned, seeing only one person stood there behind us, glaring in undisguised fury, red eyes glowing as if possessed by some demon.

"Ivanaka," I said in recognition.

"How dare you?" she screamed, spittle flying from ruby lips.

"Look," began Hillary, moving ahead of me toward the princess, "you had better stay out of the way. We're not –"

Before she could finish, Ivanaka grabbed an unplugged lamp and charged. Hillary cast about for a weapon and found a fireplace poker as I backed away. Seeing the force of Ivanaka's rush, Hillary stepped back and raised the poker above her head, but she swung back too far and pierced the portrait with it, slashing across the left leg. Ivanaka screamed in pain and fell, holding her bloody left calf. I went cold. It could not have been a coincidence, but surely there could be no connection between the portrait and princess? On a hunch, I tore at the picture's hole so that the leg separated from the body. Ivanaka let out another wild scream, worse than the last, and I turned, seeing that her left leg had been severed cleanly.

"My god." I took the poker from Hillary's hand and began to stab the portrait. With each blow, Ivanaka shrieked. Blood began to pour from every wound and she writhed on the floor in a growing pool of blood, which seemed black in the darkness. At last, after a dozen or more blows, I stopped, breath heaving, and stared at the still body of Ivanaka. For a moment, nothing moved, the only sound my labored gasping, but then the body began to grow wider and fatter. Hair turned grey, skin turned a ghastly, mottled color, and before long, the corpse looked just like the portrait I had stabbed. I turned to gaze at it and backed away in horror. The painting had mended itself, but it no longer resembled the hideous creature on the floor. Instead, Princess Ivanaka Grump stood resplendent in all her youth and beauty like she had every day I'd seen her.

"How is this possible?" I asked.

Hillary laid a comforting hand on me. The body on the floor began to putrefy at an accelerated rate, noxious fumes threatening to overcome us. "Well, she did once brag that she got her moral compass from her father."

"I guess that explains it."

"We had better get out of here before the stench is the end of us."

"Agreed."

We gingerly stepped around what remained of Princess Ivanaka, noticing that the floor had begun to crumble around her, as if her bodily fluids were some sort of acid, eating away at everything. We crept out of the room, deciding we should avoid the royal wing of the palace, as too many of the family had decided not to attend Hillary Fest. The question was where to hide.

We passed the room where Grump made his radio broadcasts, which I explained to Hillary as we paused inside it, planning our next move. She found it hard to believe there was a device that made anyone sound like him due to the risk, which she wanted to exploit for our benefit.

"Why don't we announce that we're somewhere else?" she suggested. "Everyone will go there and stop looking for us here."

"Good idea." I moved to the controls and began turning various things on, trying to figure out the system. I put the headphones on and played with a few dials before finding the right setting, which I tested in the headphones. But no sooner did I have it ready then she stopped me.

"Wait. I have an even better idea. Why don't we tell him that the attack he's been predicting from the U.C. is here and everyone should drink those vials of poison around their necks?"

I wasn't sure how to react but found myself thinking out loud. "It would kill everyone but the slaves."

"Who are the only ones who deserve to live. Everyone else is evil."

"Are they? I got most of them into this."

"And you can get them out of it," she interrupted, "just like you wanted."

"Yeah, but I didn't mean killing them."

"They want to kill you even now."

"Yeah but they've all been duped, partly with my help, and then brainwashed. That can be undone."

Hillary shook her head. "Based on what I've seen and what you've told me, they're too far gone."

"No. No, I already saved one of them. The boy, David, has been taught hate since he was born, and he's already accepted both me and Jada."

"You don't really know that. Besides, he's a kid."

"There are thousands of other kids on this island."

"And do you think a single one of them is going to give you a chance to reach them after what you just did? By rescuing me, you not only risked your life, but you just destroyed your reputation here, and without that, they'll never listen to you again."

My heart sank. She was right. As I'd already explained to her, I had used the esteem in which I was held to get through to David. I was possibly the only person these people would've listened to about how vile Grump really was before today. But my actions had cost me that and I hadn't even considered it before now. Was I the only one who could save them? Maybe not, but I'd seen the devotion to Grump everywhere. I had no doubt the adults were likely a lost cause. The kids might be, too. Still, wasn't a slim hope better than none?

Suddenly Hillary grabbed both of my wrists and, before I knew what she was doing, tied my hands behind me with an extension cord.

"Sorry about this, but it has to be done. You've told me about so many terrible plans they have to destroy the world in one way or another. They have to be stopped."

I started to protest but she gagged me.

"Can't have you making noises while I do this."

I continued protesting, more urgently, because I knew something she didn't – once she gave the order, Cue or someone else would launch the missiles and start a nuclear holocaust. But she couldn't know what caused my increased agitation and likely assumed it was more of the same protest, not a new one she needed to heed. My mind went to the detonator in my pocket. At the very least, I had to blow the control room to bits before she could do this.

Suddenly we heard a noise out in the hall as someone was looking for us. "Better hurry." She turned on the button that would let her address the entire island.

"Dear comrades," she began, "the time has come. I've been warning you that the Treasonous United Colonies means to kill us all, and I was right. Just now they have attacked and ruined Hillary Fest. They've killed a host of other comrades. Their planes are coming, carrying bombs that will destroy us all. Only I, the great emperor Donald Grump, can save you and bring you to the promised land. It is time to drink the vials you have around your neck. Don't even wait to say goodbye to your friends and family. This isn't truly goodbye but a new beginning. Join me in another new life. Drink. Drink now! Those who do not obey will be denied entrance into my new paradise, as will your friends and family! Drink!"

She stopped there and looked back at me. I furiously gestured with my hand in my pocket. Her confusion turned to resignation and she pulled off my gag.

"Untie me, quick!"

"What's the rush?"

"The detonator! I have to blow the bombs at the Golden Armory, or they'll launch nuclear missiles before drinking the poison!"

"What? Jesus."

She yanked the detonator from my pocket and fiddled with it as I hurriedly yelled directions. One screen brought up a list of items and I told her which ones to arm, then detonate. She did each and the device registered that the signals to them had been lost. Aside from that, there was no indication it had worked, and we were much too far away to have witnessed any explosions. As a result, I felt it difficult to calm down.

"Come on," I began, "untie me."

She did so, apologizing again.

"You just killed millions of people and here you are apologizing for tying me up."

She looked at me ruefully. "Point taken, but what's done is done."

"Do you think everyone did it?"

"No way to know. Let's pretend they didn't and be careful. Maybe not everyone had those. After all, the whole thing is just another con, and I doubt his family wanted to do it. Grump is probably planning to just take his wealth and get out of here."

"That would be just like him."

We went to the door, opened it, and peeked out together to see two guards lying on the floor, bodies arched painfully, mouths agape, a look of horror frozen on their faces. One man's hand stretched toward us; the empty vial clutched in it.

Worried about Jada and David, I said, "We need to get to my rooms quickly."

"Lead the way."

We broke into a careful jog, passing corpse after corpse along the way. Some were nobles and others were members of the outer party, but they had all become the same in death. All had stopped what they were doing in an instant, which we could tell from the way items had been discarded. Drinks and decanters lay spilled, fresh liquid still pooling on the floor. Half-eaten food was clutched in one hand. We sometimes passed two people holding hands in death. I noted one sycophant after another among the dead.

For a time, it seemed that no one was alive, but then we passed the first slaves, huddled together and fearful. They didn't know what to make of us, but I told them to head back to the districts and find the Underground Railroad, that it would lead them to the shore. With everyone but them dead, they could get a ship going. Then I realized they didn't need the railroad. They could just head to the port or airport. Hopefully, someone knew enough to pilot them or sail one vessel or another from Grumpland. I told them to spread the word and they took off at a run, yelling the news. I hoped they would make it.

Then we made it to my rooms. The door stood ajar and I feared it had been searched. Seeing me hesitate, Hillary just went in and began looking around, so I joined her, calling out for them. By the second time, both Jada and David stepped from within the walk-in closet, looking caught between relief and fear. Then both ran to me for a hug, babbling about guards having kicked in the door and quickly looking around before leaving. They hadn't really searched but Jada and David had remained hidden anyway.

"I was pretty sure," I began, "you wouldn't let David take the poison when we told everyone to, but I was still worried."

"What?" Jada asked. "You did that? Not Grump?"

"Hillary did, over my objections. There's no attack. We can explain later. I think we still need to get off the island immediately. There are bound to be people who know Grump didn't give the command and they're probably headed this way."

"They're already here," said Hillary from the window, where she was looking down at the road to the palace. I joined her and saw a veritable caravan of vehicles arriving. There must've been scores of armed men who hadn't killed themselves, maybe because they'd been with Grump at Hillary Fest and known His Majesty wasn't giving the order. I wondered how many in the crowd had known. Perhaps there were more survivors, but it didn't matter. The survival of the three people with me did.

"Look," I began, "I need you three to get to the Peregrine and get off the island."

"Us three? What about you?" Hillary asked.

"I'll give myself up as a distraction so you can go."

"Very noble, but no."

"Yes. And it's not noble. I'm the one who caused all of this and I'm going to finish it. Besides, only you can fly this thing. And you've got to convince the U.C. military to destroy this place. I can't do that."

Glancing out the window again, she seemed to accept that and asked, "What did you call this plane?"

"Peregrine. It's like an Osprey and there's only one. It's at the Golden Armory. You should be able to fly it and get off the island." I told her details that Svetlana had passed on to me, about its range and pressurization, and where to find it.

We heard boots downstairs and starting to spread out in search of us, the occasional scream of slaves ringing out, and sometimes gunfire.

Hillary asked, "You're sure about this?"

"Positive." I turned to Jada, unsure what to say. Her concern was plain. Suddenly she grabbed my head in both hands and passionately kissed me. I reluctantly broke it off and she took David's hand and began leading him away as I assured him the women would keep him safe. We all moved to the door.

"We have to kill Grump," Hillary insisted.

"They'll take me to him," I replied. "I'll do what I can."

"Where do you think he will be? Maybe I can get there with this plane. Did it have weapons?"

"Not that I saw. I have no idea where he'll be anyway." Then it hit me. "Wait. The pyramid. He's probably there."

"Why?"

"He may not have given the order for everyone to kill themselves, but he knows they obeyed. The next step is for him to buy his way into heaven. Most of his followers are gone. He likely thinks it's time to join them so he can continue to rule them all."

"Amazing."

"Listen. There's a landing pad at the top, which is where he'll be. Swing by and if you don't see me, get out of there." I started to move away.

"Okay. Good luck."

Hearing where the guards were, I ran in their direction as Hillary, Jada, and David went a different way, toward the palace rear. I cast one final look at them, certain I'd never see them again, and for that if nothing else, I was determined to kill Grump.

I heard guards coming up the stairs ahead of me and purposely ran past them, trying to act surprised when they saw me and gave pursuit, yelling to each other that I was wanted alive. That was a relief. I led them away from the others on a chase of five minutes before ducking into a suite of rooms that I suspected offered no way out. I was right and was soon coming out with my hands raised, a dozen armed men apprehending me.

"Where's that whore?" one asked, glaring at me.

I arched an eyebrow. "I don't know. We got separated. Said something about getting a plane at the airport. Might want to check there."

"Check it out," he barked at the others, two of whom left.

They bound my hands and forced me to march through the gilded halls and past corpse after corpse until we reached their armored vehicle. I was loaded in and driven off with an escort of two more vehicles before and after us. Along the way, cars were abandoned on the road, with dead occupants. We passed by Hillary Fest and saw an endless sea of bodies. The men with me made no secret of their hatred for me and I suspected that they would've killed me were it not for their allegiance to Grump. Somehow, he was saving my life when I was hoping to take his.

I didn't bother to ask where we were going, but I felt pleased to see the pyramid getting nearer. It proved to be our destination as we veered off the highway for it. It took ten minutes for them to get me out of the vehicle and into that huge building looming overhead, and finally up to somewhere near the top, where I was escorted all the way to that platform I'd told Hillary about, on the pyramid's rear. That's where I found Grump, who indicated to the two remaining guards beside me that my hands should be freed because he intended to make me drink the poison, a vial of which was handed to me.

Long moments of tense silence followed, with him looking down his nose at me like so many of those statues I'd seen. It was also the expression he wore when intending to kill someone. He was unarmed.

"Why'd you do it?" he finally asked.

"Do what?"

"Free the prisoner."

Most of his people were dead, but still, he focused on a blonde woman who happened to have the same first name as Hillary Minton. "I needed her to fly me off the island."

"You were leaving soon enough anyway. Another ten days."

"Yes, but I wanted to take a few people with me."

"Who? None of my people would go with you. It's paradise here."

"You're delusional, you know that? It's a nightmare here. Your Ebony Girl and one of the children were coming with me."

"And now they'll end up dead, just like you. What happened to you? You were so loyal, and now you're just a traitor. One who's about to die."

"I saw you for what you really are, and it turned my stomach."

Pouting, he said, "Everyone loves me. Everyone. And everyone says so."

I wasn't going to get into this stupid bullshit with him. "All of your supporters are dead."

Grump shrugged. "Eh. We had a good run."

"You don't care at all, do you? Do you think they're joining you in heaven?"

He laughed. "You're just as stupid as *they* are. The deal I made with Satan was that *he* gets them. The whole lot of them! But I'm going to heaven. Goodbye loser." He turned to go, started the golden escalator, but then stopped it a few feet up, looking back. "You're a total loser, you know that? I mean a total zero. Worse than zero. What's worse than zero? I don't even know."

Suddenly a roar sounded from behind him and the Peregrine soared into view, with Hillary standing in an open doorway. In one hand, she held a gun that she fired at Grump, striking him in the shoulder. He fell down the stairs and past the gold bars, which he struck his head upon before coming to rest ten feet from me. Hillary then shot at the guards, who were slow to react. She killed both in a few shots, then flashed a grin as the Peregrine seemingly landed itself on the platform. She left the craft running as she jumped out and came up to me, handing me a shotgun. I threw the poison vial on the floor, shattering it. Behind her, I saw Jada and David strapped into their seats.

"Are you okay?" Hillary yelled in my ear.

"Never better. Your timing is perfect. Who's flying that thing?"

"Auto-pilot. It has a few locations pre-programmed. This was one of them."

"Let's get out of here. Everyone's dead but him and the slaves, who should be heading for the coasts."

"I know, I just flew over more bodies than I could count. Looks like we saved the worst for last."

We turned to look at Grump, who had gotten to his knees, his hands covered in a green, slimy substance that I belatedly realized was his blood. Was he even human? Or had jealousy and greed just turned him into a monster? I didn't much care anymore and just wanted to be free. I trained my shotgun on him.

Grump had moved toward us, still on his knees. "Please, I'm begging you. Spare my life. I'll give you anything you want. We can make a deal!"

Hillary spat at him. "You wouldn't honor it anyway."

"Yeah, but we can still make one."

To Grump's right and left, the air beside him began to shimmer and turn dark like a storm cloud, little bolts of lightning crackling the air. Suddenly a figure emerged from each. On one side stood Mitch McKonnell, resplendent in his black robe and cowl, the wicked scythe gleaming. To the other stood a red figure in a sleek business suit, two horns on its head jutting into the sky with a flame burning between them, a pointed tail gently swooshing the air behind it like a relaxed feline. Grump leered at us in triumph.

"Hope you got something good in that shotgun," he began, "because you're gonna need it. Mitch! Satan! Get 'em!"

But neither of Grump's allies moved.

"Don't just stand there!" Grump shrieked.

Satan laid a hand on Grump's shoulder. "We're here for *you*, stupid."

Clearly surprised, Grump blurted out, "But we had a deal!"

Satan shrugged. "Did we? I seem to recall teaching you not to honor those."

Grump sputtered, at a loss for words. I'd heard enough anyway and decided to put an end to this. I pulled the trigger. The shotgun jumped in my hands as the blast tore into Grump's torso and head, a green mist of blood surrounding him. He fell forward and rolled over, one hand reaching for the pile of gold bars just outside his reach. His head lolled back and turned toward me, and as his eyes began to glaze over and Death raised his scythe, he croaked out one final statement.

"I beat Hillary by 100 points!"

McKonnell let the blade fall. The sound of metal slicing through bone rent the air and Grump's head rolled past me to stop near the elevator. Somehow, even in death, he still seemed petulant, whiny, entitled, and boorish. I saw movement beyond and realized that several Latino slaves were inside the elevator, cowering in fear.

Beside me, Hillary gasped, and I turned to see her pointing at Grump's headless body. Death and Satan had disappeared, but Grump's corpse had begun to tremble. Movement could be seen at his stomach, as if something rather large were inside and struggling to get out. Finally, a nasty little creature about a foot-long burst from his abdomen, razor-sharp teeth gnashing, its barbed tail slashing the air around it. With a shotgun blast, I put the parasite out of its misery.

Hillary asked, "Do you think that thing was controlling him all this time?"

"No way to know. I think that would be giving Grump too much of an out."

"Agreed. Let's not mention it."

She started for the aircraft, but I had a thought and paused. I walked over to the gold bars and, on a hunch, scratched the surface of one. The gold plating came off, revealing bronze beneath it.

"Just as I thought," I muttered, turning away.

We leapt back into the Peregrine, the Latino slaves eagerly joining us when I gestured for them to, and we lifted off. As we rose above the land, a green cloud of death swept from doorway to field, rushing over land and sea alike. While humanity had already been purged, the cloud struck down the animals and those beasts of Dr. Karson's creation. They fled before it, some taking to the sky, but tendrils of green smoke lashed out to ensnare them, pulling them plummeting back to Earth. Jada clutched at me, fearing we would not escape, but in the ultimate sign of our goodness and the righteousness of our souls, the dread gas touched us not. We made for the coast in the distance, eager to be free of this wretched place.

Like Atlantis before it, Grumpland began to disappear beneath the ocean surface. As rescue ships arrived, many of the slaves were pulled to freedom, having been untouched by the noxious green gas. Anyone white was assumed to be a Grump loyalist who should perish beneath the waves. Their cries for help went unheeded. A few feared death so strongly that they committed the ultimate sin and claimed to be captured Democrats, but they were unable to show the brand proving this, nor any scars from their backs being lashed. They finally drowned gurgling Grump's name as the sea began to boil and lightning lashed the sky. Then a great leviathan of unspeakable hideousness rose from the depths to swallow Grumpland. The Latinos with us were heard to cry out in Spanish, "Reimponer! Reimponer!"

"What does that mean?" I asked, staring as the huge creature's gaping maw, full of razor-sharp teeth, began to close around the island.

"To restore!" one cried out, pointing at the leviathan. "The creature restores!"

Indeed, it seemed true. The fantastic beast I've dubbed Reimponyr cracked the island into bits with one mighty bite, then slurped it all down in a violent rush of thrashing, frothing waves. The monster swept the last remnants of Grumpism from Earth as it vanished beneath the sea, which grew still and silent. The clouds parted as a warm shower fell to cleanse us all, sunlight beaming down on us, a rainbow appearing in sky over where Grumpland had once stained the Earth.

Epilogue

Nine months have passed since that fateful day, which resounded with the world. Hillary piloted us to Andrews Air Force Base outside Washington, D.C., while many ships had rescued the slaves and brought them ashore. Each was given a favorable immigration status and allowed a chance at a new life, much as I had been.

I write from the home that I now share with David, my adopted son, and Jada, who carries my child. David has been a work in progress. I waited until he was ready before telling him that the land we lived in was that Treasonous United Colonies he'd heard so many awful things about. By then, he'd come to find it the wonderful place of opportunity that all immigrants dream of it to be. His shock passed quickly, and fear made no appearance. After this, his rejection of all things Grumpian came swiftly, for his entire life had been a lie. We homeschooled him, Jada and I, for there was much to be caught up on and he was still, even now, not ready to join the kids who'd spent their lives in normal surroundings. One day soon, that will change.

Naturally, he was curious for an explanation about those lies and what had led to the existence of Grumpland, so I told him a story of my own making called *The Green Emperor* story, the title a spoof on *The Golden Emperor* that Ivanaka had tried to read to children on the day I met him.

"The Green Emperor"

Once upon a time, many people came in ships to the shores of a new land. They were leaving a country where most of them were not as free and happy as they would've liked. The reason was that laws and other such things did not apply equally to all people, including them. It wasn't fair and they didn't like it.

So, some of the great men among them founded a new country on those shores. They called it the United Colonies of Amnesia. When creating the United Colonies, they drafted documents called the Declaration of Independence and the Constitution, which declared among other things that all people are free and created equal. The way things were to work, no one was supposed to have so much power that anyone else suffered for it. This was achieved with something called a government, which all countries have. But not all governments are the same.

The men who founded the United Colonies created a new type of government, or republic, which was divided into three equal branches, so that no branch could dominate the others and ruin the freedom that citizens wanted and deserved. In time, the world would come to rejoice in this Dream of the Republic, which spread far and wide. This dream inspired many countries to become like the U.C., or their people to travel there to become a citizen.

But not everyone was happy. Despite the founding claims, all were not equal in the United Colonies. White, heterosexual men and the women who loved them were in power. And many of them owned slaves, who had no freedoms at all. Other injustices abounded. Stories of the resulting suffering spread far and wide, sometimes in books, often in the news, and later in films and TV. With each story, awareness of these injustices changed hearts and minds, leading many to demand changes to the laws to match their views. To them, a conflict existed between the Dream of the Republic and the reality of the republic. And when their voices grew loud enough that they could be denied no longer, change happened, social outcry by social outcry, right by right, law by law. Satisfaction with the republic grew.

And yet still not everyone was happy. Some people wanted to conserve what had come before, so that nothing ever changed, for they believed that the original reality of the republic had been right all along and that every change brought about a tarnishing of the dream's golden appeal. They felt that their country was being taken from them with every shift. Their values were no longer championed, but threatened. New arrivals on the land's shores put their positions of power at risk. Their livelihood suffered, their prospects dimmed, and their fortunes fell. And they blamed it all on those liberals who sought to change the reality of the republic to match its dream. The disparity had put the citizens of the country on a collision course.

Now change is a thing that few people like, and yet change is life's only constant. And yet still do people cling to a present that the tide of change threatens to wash away. And they lament a past that is long gone but which they fantasize of restoring, like a tarnished dream that one can burnish back to golden beauty with enough effort. Hatred grew in their hearts.

Hatred for their losses. Hatred for the changes. Hatred for those who'd brought those changes about.

Some in power courted this hatred, enriching themselves on it like carrion birds feeding on the bloated corpse of a dying dream. They crowed lies to all who would hear. Lies about how those who sought change were destroying the country. Lies that liberals were destroying their lives. Lies that they were destroying their freedoms. Exaggerations flew. Hyperbole blossomed. Deceit reigned supreme.

They said that someone was to blame. And they were evil. They were corrupt. They were elitists having the audacity to tell them, the good, decent, hardworking people of this country, who rightfully belonged here, how to think, and how to believe, and how to live. These evil people were outsiders, newcomers, immigrants all. They'd come to these shores for the Dream of the Republic, found it wanting, and caused changes that harmed those who'd called the United Colonies home for far longer. How dare they? This was a conspiracy to destroy the country, and liberals in that country were the cause! They were committing treason!

One day, a wealthy man named Grump came before these conservatives and spoke of his hatred, too. He told them he could restore the country and their Dream of the Republic if only they made him their leader. No one would be allowed in anymore. He'd build a wall to keep them out and repeal laws that had taken favors from them and given them to these unworthy newcomers. He was a vile man, corrupt, twisted, dishonest, greedy, jealous of everyone, and ugly to his core. Even his supporters knew this, but he told them what they wanted to hear. And on a tide of hate, he swept into the Presidency, the most powerful position in the United Colonies, and laid waste to much that he found, just as his followers desired.

But Grump could not change enough of what these "Republicans" wanted, even with powerful lawmakers by his side, for the rule of law stopped him. Democracy and the other branches of government that the founding fathers had created stood in his way, as did the liberal "Democrats" who had so long pushed for and achieved change. He and Republicans agreed – the United Colonies government had to be torn down and replaced by a monarchy with Grump as its king amid one-party rule. He even called in help from foreign powers as a red malaise overcame conservatives, who were so desperate that they welcomed foreign interference in how their country worked. Democrats called this treason, and Republicans called the changes that Democrats had long been putting in place the same.

Grump tried to get what he and his supporters wanted by shattering norms of common decency, truthfulness, integrity, accountability, and more. They cheered, for he was angering those who'd ruined their Dream of the Republic, and their hate was so fierce that they cared not at all that he was worse than any politician who'd ever come before. As long as he lived up to a promise... to destroy all that they hated. They looked the other way when he destroyed all that was good, for in their hatred, they had become lost, clinging to a Dream of the Republic that was near to death.

He told them that all of his behavior was okay, that only the favorable stories about him were to be believed. All others were fake, and those who told such stories were out to destroy him and therefore them. Democrats were enemies. Change was not inevitable, but a cancer evil people had caused and spread to destroy the hearts, minds, and souls of people who want things to remain the same. And his supporters believed, for he knew how to lie to those who are eager for it.

Plant a fear, sow a doubt, intimate a secret plot, and conspiracy will roar through them like a scythe through wheat, hacking down their minds to little stubs that cannot process common sense, wisdom, or intelligence. A Grumpian Scythe exceeds all others in this regard, and he who wields it knew his victims from before he left swaddling clothes, for despite the gold breast in his mouth, he was like them all along, just as he claimed – feed on a hearty diet of lies from the Suckled Teat of Self-Delusion and like puppets on a string will they follow, loyal to the last, unto villainy.

Try as he might, Grump failed to destroy the Constitution and the United Colonies along with it. Democracy withstood the Grumpian Charge, which didn't lay waste to the halls of power. The U.C. Presidency does not last forever, and while Grump tried to extend it and make himself a Golden Emperor, he could not.

And so, with his supporters cheering him on, he founded a new country, Grumpland, far out into the sea, where he declared himself emperor and Made Grumpland Great for himself and his Inner Party – those people who'd helped him con his followers into accepting, even welcoming every abuse he championed. They left the United Colonies in droves, the wealthiest joining the lesser Outer Party, but most being ordinary members of the working class, the proletariat. And all those liberal Democrats they hated were not allowed in, not unless they were captured and brought to slavery for the exaltation of the white, heterosexual men and the women who loved them. With scythian words, he imprisoned his followers in a shroud of lies once more, that he would deliver all their dreams if they only loved him. If only they were loyal. And so, they were. He'd become the Green Emperor, stealing from his own people to enrich only himself.

Back in the United Colonies, with the most radical Republicans gone from the land, sanity resurfaced among those Republicans that had remained. They came to see at last that their values could survive in a changing landscape of morality that still held a place for them, should they take it. Rather than demanding others to comply with their world view, they recognized that they could only offer it and bring into the fold those to whom it appealed. Democrats welcomed back their counterparts in civility, cooperation, and compromise, each and every one recognizing that no one gets everything that they want, nor should they, for to gorge on satisfaction is to die of satiation. There can be no longing, no striving, no growth in the heart or mind this way, only stagnation, decay, and death.

For liberals, despite all the change they had wrought, it had often seemed that two steps forward toward fairness and justice for all had met with one step backward. In the Age of Grump, it had become a thousand steps backward. And so, with him gone from their shores, as the world once again looked to the United Colonies, its leader in freedom and morality, kindness with might, trust and nurturing, the time had come for ten thousand steps forward.

Reimponyr had come.

Democracy had won.

Far away in Grumpland, the Green Emperor grew restless in this prison of his own making. Consumed by hatred, driven by jealousy and greed, Grump grew increasingly mad. Having long used his scythe on his followers, he made them accept every story he told them about how the Treasonous United Colonies had wronged all of them, and that only he could set it right. And if, as God's Chosen One, he somehow failed, they could drink the poisoned wine he gave them and join him in the afterlife, where they would finally get their every heart's desire.

And in the end, that was all that they could hope for, as the fateful day came when they drank his poisoned wine just as they'd imbibed every other harmful elixir he'd poured for them. They died happily alongside him, believing that a world that had long gone on without them awaited anew.

The "Ben Karson" Recipe

This drink is reputed to prevent homosexuality and other forms of sexual deviation if consumed monthly, but banding of the liquids is required. This is very important (see "The Morjekstein" Variant, aka, the warning below)! Either that or they must be consumed in rapid succession, and in the proper order (listed) as a series of shots. The Jolly Roger should be repeatedly crushed between the teeth and swallowed as a final step.

1. Red
   a. 1 oz fresh blood extracted from the small, erect penis of a virile, heterosexual man.
   b. Substitutes: bloody Mary mixer, red Gatorade, or red zinfandel
2. Orange
   a. 1 oz unsweetened OJ, freshly squeezed, with pulp
3. Yellow
   a. 1 oz fresh sperm from a virile heterosexual man with a small penis (preferably same man as the red portion)
   b. 2 drops yellow food coloring.
   c. Substitutes (for sperm): milk or creamer from a heterosexual cow
4. Green
   a. 1 oz water from a pure spring
5. Blue
   a. 1 oz blue curaçao

6. Purple
    a. Purple drank
        i. 1 oz vodka (preferably of Russian origin)
        ii. 1 oz purple cough syrup
        iii. 1 Jolly Roger candy, preferably phallic-shaped

"The Morjekstein" Variant

If the liquids are allowed to mix, they cause homosexuality or make those who are already homosexual even more so (i.e., in homosexual parlance, they become "flaming"). When milk or creamer substitute is used for yellow, it should be from a homosexual cow. As a final step, the Jolly Roger should be sucked on continuously until dissolved.

Publisher's Note: it is not recommended to consume bodily fluids. Please use the suggested substitutes.

About the Author

Buck Wilde writes books. With words. Lots of them. They're good, too. Everyone should go buy his stuff.

Connect with him online at fb.me/BuckWildeMan